I0639529

James Henry Kyner

Odes, Hymns and Songs of the G. A. R

James Henry Kyner

Odes, Hymns and Songs of the G. A. R

ISBN/EAN: 9783744778411

Printed in Europe, USA, Canada, Australia, Japan

Cover: Foto ©Andreas Hilbeck / pixelio.de

More available books at **www.hansebooks.com**

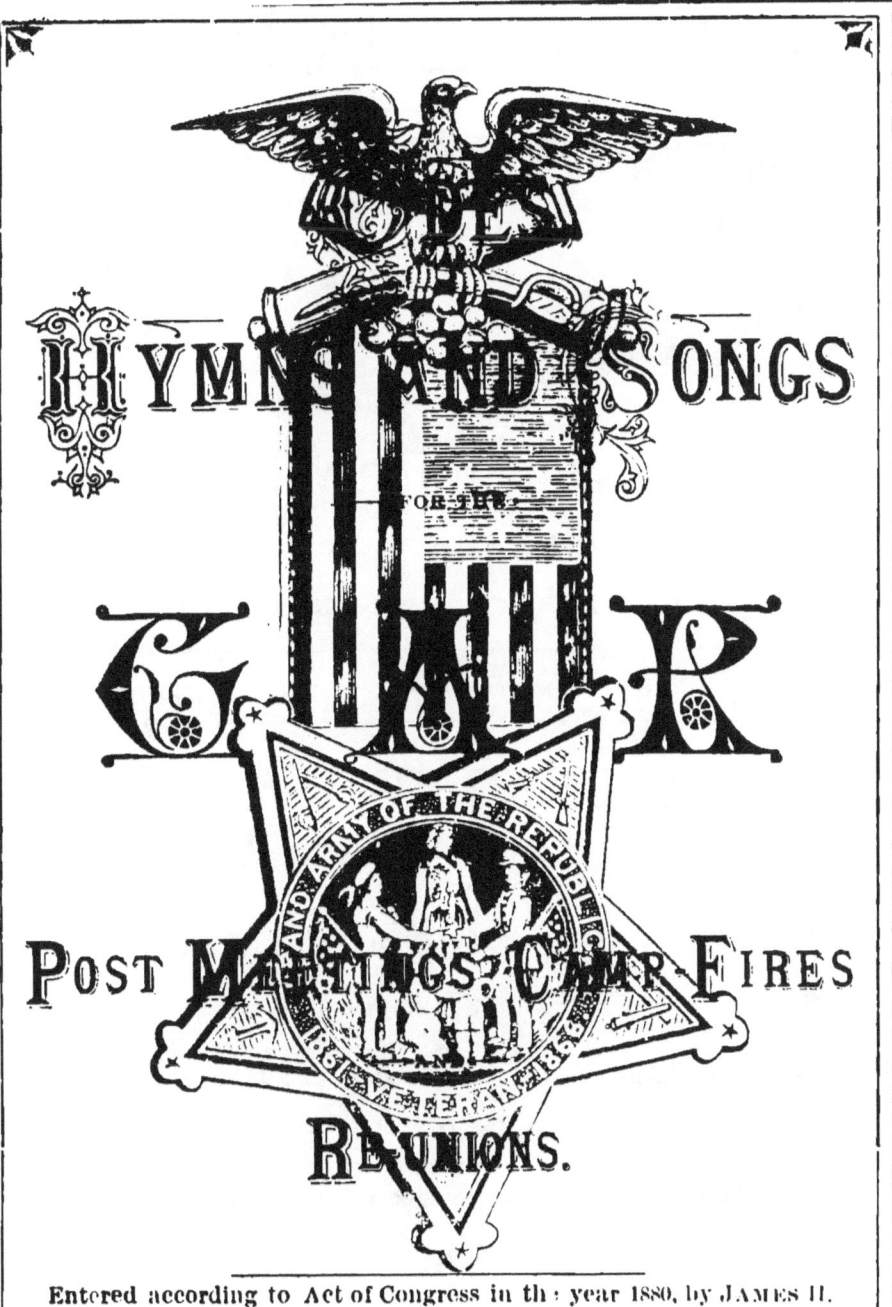

HYMNS AND SONGS

FOR THE

G. A. R.

POST MEETINGS, CAMP-FIRES

RE-UNIONS.

Entered according to Act of Congress in the year 1880, by JAMES H. KYNER, in the office of the Librarian of Congress at Washington.

HYMNS AND SONGS

OF THE

G. A. R.

Bur Kundred Popular Old Ballads of the War:

SONGS THAT WERE

SUNG ON THE MARCH, AROUND THE CAMP-FIRE, AND IN THE PRISON, BY THE LOYAL MEN OF FREEDOM'S GRAND ARMY.

COMPILED AND PUBLISHED BY

Comrade JAMES H. KYNER,

Of Geo. A. Custer Post No. 7, Dept. of Neb., G. A. R.

OMAHA, NEB.:
HENRY GIBSON, HERALD PRINTING AND BINDING ESTABLISHMENT.

1880.

ODES, HYMNS AND SONGS

OF THE

GRAND ARMY OF THE REPUBLIC

OPENING ODE.

(Air—"Home Again.")

Once again, once again, Comrades here we meet,
And gath'ring round the kindling fire,
Our words of cheer repeat.
'Tis here remembrance fills the cup,
'Tis here she warms the heart,
And as we hear the well known name,
Her sleeping echoes start.

CHORUS.

Once again, once again, Comrades here we meet,
And gath'ring round the kindling fire,
Our words of cheer repeat.

Happy days, happy days, Days of joy and dread,
Come sweeping thro' the vale of thought,
Like hosts to victory led.
And conq'ring all the time between,
We live the past once more,
While still the rainbow tint of hope
The future arches o'er.

GREETING ODE.

(Air—"Glory Hallelujah.")

Warm be the welcome and glad be the cheer,
Greeting our comrades who join with us here,
Warm as in days when with never a fear,
We all went marching on.

CHORUS.
Glory, glory, Hallelujah,
Glory, glory, glory Hallelujah,
Glory, glory, Hallelujah,
We all go marching on.

Held by fraternity in bonds that are sure,
Drawn close in charity by ties that are pure,
Filled with a loyalty that ever shall endure,
We still go marching on.

CHORUS.—Glory, glory, Hallelujah, &c.

Elbow to elbow we stood through the fight,
Elbow to elbow we stand here to-night,
Elbow to elbow 'till heaven is in sight.
We all go marching on.

CHORUS.—Glory, glory, Hallelujah, &c.

MUSTER-IN ODE.

(Air—"America.")

My country 'tis of thee,
Sweet land of liberty,
Of thee I sing;
Land where my comrades died.
Land of the pilgrims' pride,
From ev'ry mountain side,
Let freedom ring.

Our fathers, God to thee,
Author of liberty,
To thee we sing.
Long may our land be bright
With freedom's holy light,
Protect us by thy might,
Great God our King.

BADGE ODE.

(Air—"Hold the Fort.")

Comrade, take this badge of Freedom
Our Republic gives,
Let it be the sign that honor
Ever loyal lives.

CHORUS.
Wear the badge and keep it shining,
All life's journey through,
Ever as the glorious emblem
Of the work we do.

Then, proud eagle, still soar sunward;
Flag, your folds swing loose;
Love shall shield the helpless orphan.
Fill the widow's cruse.

CHORUS.—Wear the badge, &c.

Let it promise still thy country,
Manhood staunch and true,
And the star shall glisten brighter
When she calls for you!

CHORUS.—Wear the badge, &c.

CAMP-FIRE ODE.

(*Air—"Marching Along."*)

Hurrah, boys! a halt! pass it on down the road,
We'll unsling the knapsack, and cast off the load;
We're all brigadiers till the next bugle call,
So "each for himself and the Lord for us all."

CHORUS.

Light up the fires as we halt in the tramp,
Naught like the camp-fire ever cheers up the camp;
'Tis right here the soldier gets his fondest desire,
Then light up the camp-fire, comrades, light up the fire.

And now for the beans, and the hard-tack as well;
And now comes the coffee, O God, bless the smell!
The salt-junk is here, but the smell never mind,
As "each for himself," we can all go it blind.

CHORUS.—Light up the fires, &c.

And now fill the pipes, boys, and pass 'round the weed;
'Tis no time to think who's the next one to bleed,
We're comrades the same, though we stand or we fall,
We're "each for the Flag, and the Lord for us all."

CHORUS.—Light up the fires, &c.

CLOSING ODE.

(Air—"Auld Lang Syne.")

Shall we forget those far-off days,
Which made us comrades all?
Shall we forget how swift the feet
That ran at duty's call?
Shall we forget the honored dead,
That sleep beneath the sod,
Who gave their lives for liberty,
Our country and our God?

No, here we pledge fraternity,
With ev'ry human life,
That sang the songs of vict'ry won,
Or fell amid the strife;
And when at last we answer here,
As death each name shall call,
We'll leave these ranks with charity,
And loyalty to all.

STAR SPANGLED BANNER.

Oh! say, can you see by the dawn's early light,
  What so proudly we hail'd at the twilight's last gleaming;
Whose broad stripes and bright stars through the perilous
    fight,
  O'er the ramparts we watch'd, were so gallantly streaming,
And the rocket's red glare, the bombs bursting in air,
Gave proof through the night that our flag was still there,
  Oh! say, does the star-spangled banner still wave,
  O'er the land of the free, and the home of the brave?

On the shore, dimly seen through the mist of the deep,
  Where the foe's haughty host in dread silence reposes,
What is that, which the breeze o'er the towering steep,
  As it fitfully blows, half conceal'd, half discloses?
Now it catches the gleam of the morning's first beam,
In full glory reflected now shines on the stream;
  'Tis the star-spangled banner, Oh! long may it wave,
  O'er the land of the free, and the home of the brave.

And where is the band who so vauntingly swore
  That the havoc of war, and the battle's confusion,
A home and a country should leave us no more?
  Their blood has wash'd out their foul footstep's pollution.
No refuge could save the hireling and slave,
From the terror of flight or the gloom of the grave;
  And the star-spangled banner in triumph doth wave,
  O'er the land of the free, and the home of the brave.

Oh! thus be it ever when freemen shall stand
  Between their loved homes and foul war's desolation;
Bless'd with victory and peace may the Heaven-rescued land
  Praise the power that hath made and preserved us a nation;
Then conquer we must, when our cause it is just,
And this be our motto—"In God is our trust!"
  And the star-spangled banner in triumph shall wave,
  O'er the land of the free, and the home of the brave.

HYMN.

FOR DECORATION DAY, 1880.

Dedicated to the Grand Army of the Republic, by J. F. Lovering, Chaplain-in-Chief.

God of the living and the dead,
  We bow before Thy face;
Pleading thy goodness and our need,
  We supplicate Thy grace.

As in the days that once were ours,
  In camp, on march, in field,
Our strength was in Thy mighty arm—
  Thy guardian love our shield;

As when the storm of battle lowered,
  Our courage was in Thee,
And for one country and one flag,
  We fought on land and sea;

As we have mourned with aching hearts
  The love of comrades brave,
And gather here to scatter flowers
  Upon each cherished grave;

So muster back our dead that they
  With us our ranks may fill,
And stand in glad fraternity,
  Shoulder to shoulder still;

So give us faith in human right,
  In justice and in Thee,
That we may hold those once our foes
  In Christian *charity;*

So make each patriot soldier's grave
  A sacred shrine to be,
That a high altar it may prove
  Of stalwart *loyalty.*

Then when the great inspection day
Shall sound its bugle call,
· May we, in Heaven's grand parade,
Give answer one and all.

Approved, WM. EARNSHAW,
Commander-in-Chief.
J F. I OVERING,
Official, Chaplain-in-Chief.
ISAAC B. STEVENS, Adj. Gen.

WHEN JOHNNY COMES MARCHING HOME.

When Johnny comes marching home again, hurrah, hurrah!
We'll give him a hearty welcome then, hurrah, hurrah!
The men will cheer, the boys will shout!
The ladies, they will all turn out,
And we'll all feel gay,
When Johnny comes marching home.

The old church bell will peal with joy, hurrah, hurrah!
To welcome home our darling boy, hurrah, hurrah!
The village lads an ' lasses say
With roses they will strew the way,
And we'll all feel gay,
When Johnny comes marching home.

Get ready for the Jubilee, hurrah, hurrah!
We'll give the hero three times three, hurrah, hurrah!
The laurel wreath is ready now
To place upon his loyal brow,
And we'll all feel gay,
When Johnny comes marching home.

Let love and friendship, on that day, hurrah, hurrah!
Their choicest treasures then display, hurrah, hurrah!
And let each one perform some part,
To fill with joy the warrior's heart,
And we'll all feel gay,
When Johnny comes marching home.

TOUCH THE ELBOW.

Rallying Song of Martindale's Brigade, First in Porter's Division. 3d Army Corps.

Words by Brig. Gen. Martindale; Sung by the Chasseur Minstrels.

When battle's music greets the ear,
Our guns are sighted at the foe;
Then nerve the hand, and bannish fear,
And, comrades touch the elbow.

CHORUS—Touch the elbow, now my boys,
Comrades, touch the elbow,
Nerve the hand, banish fear,
Comrades, touch the elbow.

Home and country, patriots' fire,
Kindle our souls with fervid glow,
And southern traitors shall retire
When northmen touch the elbow.
CHORUS.—Touch the elbow, &c.

A cannon shot may plow the rank,
And through us strike a deadly blow,
Close up the space the ball made blank,
And, comrades touch the elbow.
CHORUS.—Touch the elbow, &c.

Though many brave men touch the sod,
And crimson heart's blood freely flow,
Shout, as their spirits soar to God,
"On, comrades! touch the elbow."
CHORUS.—Touch the elbow, &c.

Now show the rocks of which you're made,
The General signals, march! hello!
Double the quick step, First Brigade,
Charge! comrades, touch the elbow.

CHORUS—Touch the elbow, now, my boys,
Comrades, touch the elbow,
Double the quick step, First Brigade,
Charge! comrades, touch the elbow.

THE ARMY BEAN.

(*Air.—"Sweet Bye and Bye."*)

There's a spot that the soldiers all love,
The mess-tent's the place that we mean,
And the dish that we like to see there,
Is the old-fashioned white Army Bean.

CHORUS—'Tis the bean that we mean,
And we'll eat as we ne'er ate before;
The Army Bean, nice and clean,
We'll stick to our beans evermore.

Now the bean in its primitive state,
Is a plant we have all often met;
And when cooked in the old army style,
It has charms we can never forget.

CHORUS.—'Tis the bean, &c.

The German is fond of saur-kraut,
The potato is loved by the Mic,
But the soldiers have long since found out
That thro' life to our beans we should stick.

CHORUS.—'Tis the bean, &c.

REFRAIN. *Air.—"Tell Aunt Rhody."*
Beans for breakfast,
Beans for dinner,
Beans for supper,
Beans, Beans, Beans.

THE GRAND ARMY.

BY RICHARD REALF.

(Air—"My Maryland.")

From eastern sea to western shore,
    Loyally;
And breasted like the knights of yore,
    Royally;
Roused by the rebel cannon roar,
Our columns thickened more and more,
With prayers behind and faith before,
    The Union's Grand Army!

From hall and hut, from near and far,
    Readily;
We sprang unto the cry for war,
    Steadily;
Stung by the crime that we abhor,
And girded on our armor for
Deliverance of the Nation, or
    Death—the Grand Army!

Through sun and gloom, through field and flood.
    Gloriously;
We pressed our path in wounds and blood;
    Victoriously;
Graves grew beneath us where we stood—
By every vale, and mount, and wood,
They wait the reveille of God—
    From the Grand Army.

Heaven rest our comrades in their graves,
    Lovingly!
Heaven beam upon our living braves,
    Approvingly!
And O, where'er our banner waves,
Freedom shall beckon unto slaves.
So long as God protects and saves
    Us—the Grand Army!

WHO WILL CARE FOR MOTHER NOW?

Why am I so weak and weary?
  See how faint my heated breath,
All around to me seems darkness,
  Tell me, comrades, is this death?
Ah, how well I know your answer,
  To my fate I meekly bow,
If you'll only tell me truly;
  Who will care for mother now?

CHORUS—Soon with angels I'll be marching,
    With bright laurels on my brow,
  I have for my country fallen,
    Who will care for mother now?

Who will comfort her in sorrow?
  Who will dry the fallen tear,
Gently smooth the wrinkled forehead?
  Who will whisper words of cheer?
Even now I think I see her,
  Kneeling praying for me! how
Can I leave her in her anguish?
  Who will care for mother now?

                    Soon with angels, &c.

Let this knapsack be my pillow,
  And my mantle be the sky;
Hasten, comrades, to the battle,
  I will like a soldier die.
Soon with angels I'll be marching,
  With bright laurels on my brow;
I have for my country fallen,
  Who will care for mother now?

                    Soon with angels, &c.

KINGDOM COMING.

Say, darkeys, hab you seen de massa,
  Wid de muffstash on his face,
Go long de road some time dis mornin',
  Like he gwine to leab de place?
He seen a smoke way up de ribber,
  Where de Linkum gunboats lay;
He took his hat an' lef' berry sudden,
  An' I spec' he's run away.

CHORUS.

  De massa run? ha! ha!
    De darkey stay? ho ho!
  It mus' be now de kingdom comin'
    An'de year ob Jubilo!

He six foot one way, two foot tudder,
  An' he weigh tree hundred pound,
His coat so big, he couldn't pay de tailor,
  An' it won't go half way round.
He drill so much, dey call him Cap'an,
  An' he get so drefful tanned,
I spec' he try an' fool dem Yankees,
  For to tink he's contraband.

                  De massa, &c.

De darkeys feel so berry lonesome,
  Libing in de log-house on de lawn,
Dey move dar tings to massa's parlor,
  For to keep it while he's gone.
Dar's wine an' cider in de kitchen,
  An' de darkeys dey'll hab some;
I spose dey'll all be cornfiscated,
  When de Linkum sojers come.

                  De massa, &c.

De oberseer he make us trouble,
An' he dribe us round a spell;
We lock him up in de smoke-house cellar,
Wid de key trown in de well.
De whip is lost, de han'cuff broken,
But de massa'll hab his pay,
He's ole enuff, big enuff, ought to know better,
Dan to went, an' run away.

De massa, &c.

TRAMP ! TRAMP ! TRAMP !
THE PRISONER'S HOPE.

In the prison-cell I sit,
Thinking, Mother dear, of you,
And our bright and happy home, so far away;
And the tears they fill my eyes,
Spite of all that I can do,
Tho' I try to cheer my comrades and be gay.

CHORUS—Tramp, tramp, tramp! the boys are marching,
Cheer up! comrades, they will come,
And beneath the Starry Flag,
We shall breathe the air again,
Of the Free-land in our own beloved home.

In the battle-front we stood,
When their fiercest charge they made,
And they swept us off, a hundred men or more;
But, before we reached their lines,
They were beaten back dismayed,
And we heard the cry of vict'ry, o'er and o'er.

CHORUS.—Tramp, tramp, tramp! &c.

So, within the prison-cell,
We are waiting for the day
That shall come to open wide the iron door;
And the hollow eye grows bright,
And the poor heart almost gay,
As we think of seeing home and friends, once more.

CHORUS.—Tramp, tramp, tramp, &c.

2

HAIL COLUMBIA.

Hail Columbia, happy land! hail, ye heroes, heaven-born
band;
　　　Who fought and bled in Freedom's cause,
　　　Who fought and bled in Freedom's cause,
And when the storm of war was gone, enjoyed the peace
your valor won.
Let independence be our boast, ever mindful what it cost;
Ever grateful for the prize, let its altar reach the skies.

CHORUS.
Firm, united, let us be, rallying round our liberty;
As a band of brothers joined, peace and safety we shall find.

Immortal patriots, rise once more, defend your rights, de-
fend your shore.
　　　Let no rude foe, with impious hand,
　　　Let no rude foe, with impious hand,
Invade the shrine where sacred lies, of toil and blood the
well-earned prize.
While offering peace sincere and just, in heaven we place a
manly trust,
That truth and justice will prevail, and every shame of
bondage fail.
　　　CHORUS.—Firm, united, let us be, &c.

Sound, sound the trump of fame! let WASHINGTON's great
name
　　　Ring through the world with loud applause,
　　　Ring through the world with loud applause,
Let every clime to Freedom dear, listen with a joyful ear.
With equal skill and God-like-power, he govern'd in the
fearful hour,
Of horrid war! or guides, with ease, the happier time of
honest peace.
　　　CHORUS.—Firm, united, let us be, &c.

Behold the chief who now commands, again to serve his
country stands—
The rock on which the storm will beat,
The rock on which the storm wi'l beat;
But armed in virtue firm and true, his hopes are fix'd on
Heaven and you.
When hope was sinking in dismay, and glooms obscured
Columbia's day,
His steady mind, from changes free, resolved on death or
liberty.
CHORUS.—Firm, united, let us be, &c.

THE BATTLE CRY OF FREEDOM.

(RALLYING SONG.)

Yes, we'll rally round the Flag, boys, we'll rally once again,
Shouting the battle-cry of freedom!
We will rally from the hill-side, we'll gather from the plain,
Shouting the battle-cry of freedom!

CHORUS.

The Union forever! hurrah! boys, hurrah!
Down with the traitors, up with the stars!
While we rally round the flag, boys, rally once again,
Shouting the battle-cry of freedom!

We are springing to the call of our brothers gone before,
Shouting the battle-cry of freedom!
And we'll fill the vacant ranks with a million freemen more,
Shouting the battle-cry of freedom!
CHORUS —The Union forever, &c.

We will welcome to our numbers the loyal true and brave,
Shouting the battle-cry of freedom!
And although he may be poor, he hall never be a slave,
Shouting the battle-cry of freedom!
CHORUS—The Union forever, &c.

So, we're springing to the call from the East and from the West
Shouting the battle-cry of freedom!
And we'll hurl the rebel crew from the land we love the best,
Shouting the battle-cry of freedom!
CHORUS.—The Union forever, &c.

MARCHING THROUGH GEORGIA.

BY PERMISSION OF ROOT & CADY.

Bring me the good old bugle, boys! we'll sing another song—
Sing it with that spirit that will start the world along—
Sing it as we used to sing it fifty thousand strong,
   While we were marching through Georgia.

CHORUS—" Hurrah! hurrah! we bring the Jubilee!
        Hurrah! hurrah! the flag that makes you free!"
So we sing the chorus from Atlanta to the sea,
   While we were marching through Georgia.

How the darkies shouted when they heard the joyful sound!
How the turkeys gobbled which our commissary found!
How the sweet potatoes even started from the ground,
   While we were marching through Georgia.
                        Hurrah, hurrah! &c.

Yes, and there were Union men who wept with joyful tears,
When they saw the honored flag they had not seen for years;
Hardly could they be restrained from breaking off in cheers,
   While we were marching through Georgia.
                        Hurrah, hurrah! &c.

"Sherman's dashing Yankee boys will never reach the coast!"
So the saucy rebels said, and 'twas a handsome boast,
Had they not forgot, alas, to reckon with the host,
   While we were marching through Georgia.
                        Hurrah, hurrah! &c.

So we made a thoroughfare for Freedom and her train,
Sixty miles in latitude—three hundred to the main;
Treason fled before us, for resistance was in vain,
   While we were marching through Georgia.
                        Hurrah, hurrah! &c.

But the march is not yet finished, nor will we yet disband,
While still a trace of treason remains to curse the land,
Or any foe against the flag uplifts a threatening hand,
   For we've been marching through Georgia.
                        Hurrah, hurrah! &c.

When Right is in the White House and Wisdom in her seat,
The reconstructed Senators and Congressmen to greet,
Why then we may stop marching, and rest our weary feet,
   For we've been marching through Georgia.
                        Hurrah, hurrah! &c.

BATTLE HYMN OF THE REPUBLIC.

BY MRS. JULIA WARD HOWE.

(*Air—"John Brown."*)

Mine eyes have seen the glory of the coming of the Lord;
He is trampling out the vintage where the grapes of wrath
are stored;
He hath loosed the fateful lightning of His terrible swift
sword;
His truth is marching on.

I have seen Him in the watch-fires of a hundred circling
camps;
They have builded Him an altar in the evening dews and
damps;
I have read His righteous sentence in the dim and flaring
lamps;
His day is marching on.

I have read a fiery gospel, writ in burnished rows of steel:
"As ye deal with my contemners, so with you my grace
shall deal;
Let the Hero, born of woman, crush the serpent with his
heel,
Since God is marching on."

He has sounded forth the trumpet that shall never call re-
treat;
He is sifting out the hearts of men before His judgment
seat;
O be swift, my soul, to answer Him! be jubilant, my feet!
Our God is marching on.

In the beauty of the lillies Christ was born across the sea,
With a glory in his bosom that transfigures you and me;
As He died to make men holy, let us die to make men free,
While God is marching on.

THE RED, WHITE AND BLUE.

Oh, Columbia, the Gem of the Ocean,
  The home of the Brave and the Free;
The Shrine of each Patriot's devotion,
  A world offers Homage to Thee!
Thy mandates make Heroes assemble,
  When Liberty's form stands in view;
Thy banners make tyranny tremble,
  When borne by the Red, White and Blue.

CHORUS.
When borne by the Red, White and Blue,
When borne by the Red, White and Blue,
Thy Banners make Tyranny tremble,
When borne by the Red, White and Blue.

When war waged its wide desolation,
  And threatened our land to deform,
The Ark then of Freedom's foundation,
  Columbia rode safe through the storm.
With her garland of victory o'er her,
  When so proudly she bore her bold crew,
With her Flag proudly floating before her,
  The boast of the Red, White and Blue.

CHORUS.—The boast of the Red, &c.

The wine cup, the wine cup bring hither,
  And fill you it up to the brim;
May the wreath they have won never wither,
  Nor the star of their glory grow dim!
May the service united ne'er sever,
  And hold to their colors so true!
The Army and Navy forever!
  Three cheers for the Red, White and Blue!

CHORUS.—Three cheers for the Red, &c.

JUST BEFORE THE BATTLE, MOTHER.

Just before the battle, mother,
I'm thinking most of you,
While upon the field, we're watching,
With the enemy in view.
Comrades brave are round me lying,
Filled with thoughts of home and God;
For, well they know that, on the morrow,
Some may sleep beneath the sod.

CHORUS.
Farewell! Mother, you may never
Press me to your heart again,
But oh! you'll not forget me, Mother,
If I'm numbered with the slain!

Oh! I long to see you, Mother,
And the loving ones at home;
But I'll never leave our Banner,
Till in honor I can come.
Tell the traitors, all around you,
That their cruel words, we know,
In ev'ry battle kill our soldiers,
By the help they give the foe.

CHORUS.—Farewell! Mother, &c.

Hark! I hear the bugle sounding;
'Tis the signal for the fight,
Now may God protect us, Mother,
As he ever does the right!
Hear the " Battle-cry of Freedom,"
How it swells upon the air!
Oh! yes, we'll rally round our Standard,
Or we'll perish nobly there!

CHORUS.—Farewell! Mother, &c.

JUST AFTER THE BATTLE.

Still upon the field of battle
I am lying, mother dear,
With my wounded comrades, waiting
For the morning to appear.
Many sleep to waken never
In this world of strife and death;
And many more are faintly calling,
With their feeble dying breath.

CHORUS.
Mother dear, your boy is wounded,
And the night is drear with pain;
But still I feel that I shall see you,
And the dear old home again.

Oh! the first great charge was fearful!
And a thousand brave men fell,
Still, amid the dreadful carnage,
I was safe from shot and shell;
So, amid the fatal shower,
I had nearly passed the day,
When, here, the dreaded Minnie struck me,
And I sunk amid the fray!

CHORUS.—Mother dear, &c.

Oh! the glorious cheer of triumph,
When the foemen turned and fled,
Leaving us the field of battle,
Strewn with dying and with dead!
Oh! the torture and the anguish
That I could not follow on;
But, here amid my fallen comrades,
I must wait till morning's dawn.

CHORUS.—Mother dear, &c.

THE BATTLE CRY OF FREEDOM.

(BATTLE-SONG.)

We are marching to the field, boys, we are going to the fight,
Shouting the battle-cry of freedom.
And we bear the glorious stars for the Union and the right,
Shouting the battle-cry of freedom.

CHORUS.
The Union forever, hurrah! boys, hurrah!
Down with the traitors, up with the stars,
For we're marching to the field, boys, going to the
fight,
Shouting the battle-cry of freedom!

We will meet the rebel host,boys,with fearless hearts and true,
Shouting the battle-cry of freedom,
And we'll show what Uncle Sam has for loyal men to do,
Shouting the battle-cry of freedom.

CHORUS.—The Union forever, &c.

If we fall amid the fray, boys, we'll face them to the last,
Shouting the battle cry of freedom.
And our comrades brave shall hear us, as they go rushing past,
Shouting the battle-cry of freedom,

CHORUS.—The Union forever, &c.

Yes, for Liberty and Union we're springing to the fight,
Shouting the battle-cry of freedom,
And the victory shall be ours, for we're rising in our might,
Shouting the battle-cry of freedom.

CHORUS.—The Union forever, &c.

SHERMAN'S MARCH TO THE SEA.

BY ADJUTANT BYERS, FIFTH IOWA CAVALRY.

Our camp fires shone bright on the mountain
That frowned on the river below,
While we stood by our guns in the morning,
And eagerly watched for the foe.
When a rider came out from the darkness
That hung over mountain and tree,
And shouted, "boys, up and be ready,
For Sherman will march to the sea!"
CHORUS—Then sang we a song for our chieftain,
That echoed o'er river and lea,
And the stars in our banner shown brighter
When Sherman marched down to the sea.

Then cheer upon cheer for bold Sherman
Went up from each valley and glen,
And the bugles re-echoed the music
That came from the lips of the men.
For we knew that the stars in our banner
More bright in their splendor would be,
And that blessings from North-land would greet us
When Sherman marched down to the sea.
CHORUS.—Then sang we a song, &c.

Then forward, boys, forward to battle,
We marched on our wearisome way,
And we stormed the wild hills of Resaca,
God bless those that fell on that day,
Then Kennesaw dark in its glory
Frowned down on the Flag of the Free,
But the east and the west bore our standard,
When Sherman marched down to the sea.
CHORUS.—Then sang we a song, &c.

Still onward we pressed till our banners
Swept out from Atlanta's grim walls,
And the blood of the Patriots dampened
The soil where the traitors' flag falls.
But we paused not to weep for the fallen,
Who slept by each river and tree,
Yet we twined them a wreath of the laurel,
And Sherman marched down to the sea.
CHORUS.—Then sang we a song, &c.

Proud, proud was our army that morning
  That stood by the Cyprus and Pine;
When Sherman said, " Boys you are weary
  This day fair Savannah is mine!"
Then sang we a song for our chieftain,
  That echoed o'er river and lea,
And the stars in our banner shown brighter
  When Sherman marched down to the sea.
    CHORUS.—Then sang we a song, &c.

A THOUSAND YEARS.

Lift up your eyes, desponding freemen!
  Fling to the winds your needless fears!
He who unfurled your beauteous banner,
  Says it shall wave a th usand years!

CHORUS—"A thousand years!" my own Co'umbia!
  'Tis the glad day so long foretold!
'Tis the gla morn whose early twilight
  Washington saw in times of old.

Tell the great world these blessed tidings!
  Yes, and be sure the bondman hears;
Tell the oppress'd of ev'ry nation,
  Jubilee lasts a thousand years!
    CHORUS.—"A thousand years!" &c.

Envious foes beyond the ocean!
  Little we heed your threat'ning sneers;
Little will they—our children's children—
  When you are gone a thousand years.
    CHORUS.—"A thousand years!" &c.

Rebels at home! go hide your faces—
  Weep for your crimes with bitter tears;
You could not bind the blessed daylight,
  Though you should strive a thousand years.
    CHORUS.—"A thousand years!" &c.

Haste thee along, thou glorious Noonday!
  Oh, for the eyes of ancient seers!
Oh, for the faith of Him who reckons
  Each of his days a thousand years!
    CHORUS.—"A thousand years!" &c.

ON! ON! ON!

A SEQUEL TO "TRAMP, TRAMP, TRAMP."

Oh! the day it came at last,
  When the glorious tramp was heard,
And the boys came marching fifty thousand strong,
  And we grasped each other's hands,
    Though we uttered not a word,
As the booming of our cannon rolled along.

CHORUS—On, on, on, the boys came marching,
    Like a grand majestic sea;
And they dashed away the guard from the heavy iron door,
    And we stood beneath the starry banner free.

Oh! the feeblest heart grew strong,
  And the most despondent sure,
When we heard the thrilling sounds we loved so well,
  For we knew that want and woe
    We no longer should endure,
When the hosts of freedom reached our prison cell.

CHORUS—On, on, on, the boys came marching,
    Like a grand majestic sea;
And they dashed away the guard from the heavy iron door,
    And we stood beneath the starry banner free.

Oh! the war is over now,
  And we're safe at home again,
And the cause we've fought and suffered for is won;
  But we never can forget,
    'Mid our woes and 'mid our pain,
How the glorious Union boys came tramping on.

CHORUS—Yes, yes, yes, the boys came marching,
    Like a grand majestic sea;
And they dashed away the guard from the heavy iron door,
    And we stood beneath the starry banner free.

Oh! 'twas Grant who led them on
  When they came to set us free,
And we glory in the sound of his dear name,
    That has dear and dearer grown
      To the ears of such as we,
Since to let us out of prison down he came.

CHORUS—Grant and the boys came onward marching,
　　Like a grand majestic sea,
And they dashed away the guard from the heavy iron door,
　　And we stood beneath the starry banner free.

OLD SHADY.

Oh! yah yah! darkies laugh wid me,
　　For de white folks say, ole Shady's free,
So don't you see that the jubilee
　　Is coming, coming, hail mighty day!

CHORUS—Den away, away, for I can't wait any longer.
　　Hooray, hooray, I'm going home.—*Repeat.*

Oh, massa got scared and so did his lady,
　　Dis child breaks for Uncle Aby,
Open de gates out here's old Shady,
　　A coming, coming, hail mighty day.
　　　CHORUS.—Den away, away, &c.

Good bye Massa Jeff, good by Miss'r Stephens,
　　'Scuse dis nigger for takin' his leavens;
'Spect pretty soon you'll hear Uncle Abram's
　　Coming, coming, hail mighty day.
　　　CHORUS.—Den away, away, &c.

Good bye, hard work, wid neber any pay,
　　I's gwin up North where the good folks say
Dat white wheat bread and a dollar a day
　　Are a coming, coming, hail mighty day.
　　　CHORUS.—Den away, away, &c.

Oh! I've got a wife, and I've got a baby,
　　Living up yonder in lower Canaday;
Won't dey laugh when dey see ole Shady,
　　Coming, coming, hail mighty day.
　　　CHORUS.—Den away, away, &c.

THE FADED COAT OF BLUE.

My brave lad he sleeps
    In his faded coat of blue,
In a lonely grave unknown;
    'Tis the heart that beat so true;
He sank faint and hungry,
    Among the famished brave,
And they laid him sad and lonely
    Within his nameless grave.

CHORUS—No more the bugle calls the weary one,
    Rest, noble spirit, in thy grave unknown;
    I'll find you, and know you,
      Among the good and true,
    When a robe of white is given
      For the faded coat of blue.

He cried, "Give me water,
    And just a little crumb,
And my mother she will bless you
    Through all the years to come;
Oh! tell my sweet sister,
    So gentle, good and true,
That I'll meet her up in heaven,
    In my faded coat of blue."

    CHORUS.—No more the bugle, &c.

He said, my dear comrades,
    You cannot take me home,
But you'll mark my grave for mother,
    She'll find me if she'll come;
I fear she'll not know me,
    Among the good and true,
When I meet her up in heaven,
    In my faded coat of blue.

    CHORUS.—No more the bugle, &c.

Long, long years have vanished,
  And though he comes no more,
Yet my heart will startling beat,
  With each foot-fall at my door;
I gaze o'er the hill
  Where he waved a last adieu.
But no gallant lad I see,
  In his faded coat of blue.

    CHORUS.—No more the bugle, &c.

No sweet voice was there,
  Breathing soft a mother's prayer,
But ther's one who takes the brave
  And the true in tender care.—
No stone marks the sod,
  O'er my lad so brave and true,
In his lonely grave he sleeps,
  In his faded coat of blue.

GOOD BYE OLD ARM.

They bore him gently from the field,
  His bleeding wounds they dressed,
And kindly gave a soothing draught
  To lull his pain to rest,
He knew the worst, that shattered arm
  No skill could e'er restore,
He heard its doom, sleep came at last,
  He felt and heard no more.
CHORUS—Good bye, old arm, my strong right arm,
    'Twas once my pride to wield,
  'Twill never bear the sword again,
    My country's flag to shield.
Oh! native land, Oh! hallow'd soil,
  The birth-place of the free,
Had I a dozen arms like this
  I would give them all to thee;
I long to wave my glit'ring sword,
  To meet the rebel foe,
But I've no arm to do it now—
  Alas! why is it so?

    CHORUS.—Good bye, old arm, &c.

THE POOR OLD SLAVE.

'Tis just one year ago to-day,
  That I remember well,
I sat down by poor Nelly's side,
  A story she did tell;
'Twas about a poor unhappy slave
  That lived for many a year,
But now he's dead and in his grave,
  No master does he fear.

CHORUS.
  The poor old slave has gone to rest,
    We know that he is free,
  Disturb him not but let him rest
    Way down in Tennessee.

She took my arm, we walked along
  Into an open field,
And she paused to breathe awhile,
  Then to his grave did steal.
She sat down by that little mound,
  And softly whispered there,
Come to me, father, 'tis thy child,
  Then gently dropped a tear.
    CHORUS.—The poor old slave, &c.

But since that time how things have changed,
  Poor Nelly that was my bride,
Is laid beneath the cold grave sod,
  With her father by her side.
I planted there upon her grave,
  The weeping willow tree,
I bathed its roots with many a tear
  That it might shelter me.
    CHORUS.—The poor old slave, &c.

AMERICA.

My country 'tis of thee,
Sweet land of liberty,
  Of thee I sing;
Land where our fathers died,
Land of the pilgrim's pride,
From every mountain side,
  Let Freedom ring.

My native country, thee,
Land of the noble free—
  Thy name I love;
I love thy rocks and rills,
Thy woods and templed hills;
My heart with rapture thrills
  Like that above.

Let music swell the breeze,
And ring from all the trees,
  Sweet freedom's song;
Let mortal tongues awake,
Let all that breathe partake,
Let rocks their silence break,
  The sound prolong.

Our father's God to thee,
Author of Liberty,
  To thee I sing;
Long may our land be bright
With freedom's holy light;
Protect us by thy might,
  Great God, our King.

WRAP THE FLAG AROUND ME, BOYS.

Oh, wrap the flag around me boys,
  To die were far more sweet,
With freedom's starry emblem, boys,
  To be my winding sheet.
In life I loved to see it wave,
  And follow where it led,
And now my eyes grow dim, my hands
  Would clasp its last bright shred.

CHORUS.

Then wrap the flag around me, boys,
  To die were far more sweet,
With freedom's starry emblem, boys,
  To be my winding sheet,

Oh, I had thought to greet you, boys,
  On many a well-won field,
When to our starry banner, boys,
  The trait'rous foe should yield,
But now alas I am denied
  My dearest earthly prayer;
You'll follow and you'll meet the foe,
  But I shall not be there.

CHORUS.—Then wrap the flag, &c.

But tho' my body moulder, boys,
  My spirit will be free,
And every comrade's honor, boys,
  Will still be dear to me.
There in the thick and bloody fight,
  Ne'er let your ardor lag,
For I'll be there still hovering near
  Above the dear old flag.

CHORUS.—Then wrap the flag, &c.

THE VACANT CHAIR.

We shall meet, but we shall miss him;
  There will be one vacant chair;
We shall linger to caress him,
  While we breathe our evening prayer.
When, a year ago, we gathered,
  Joy was in his mild blue eye;
But a Golden cord is severed,
  And our hopes in ruins lie.

CHORUS.

We shall met, but we shall miss him:
  There will be one vacant chair;
We shall linger to caress him,
  While we breathe our evening prayer.

At our fireside, sad and lonely,
  Often will the bosom swell
At remembrance of the story
  How our noble Willie fell;
How he strove to bear our banner
  Through the thickest of the fight,
And upheld our country's honor,
  In the strength of manhood's might.

CHORUS.—We shall meet, &c.

True, they tell us wreaths of glory
  Ever more will deck his brow;
But this soothes the anguish only,
  Sweeping o'er the heart strings now.
Sleep to-day, O early fallen!
  In thy green and narrow bed;
Dirges from the pine and cypress
  Mingle with the tears we shed.

CHORUS.—We shall meet, &c.

ANSWER TO "WHO WILL CARE FOR MOTHER NOW?"

Quell, oh, quell your fears my darling,
  Think not of your mother, child;
Though I never cease my weeping,
  Though my thoughts are fierce and wild,
I will try to bear up nobly,
  To God's decree humbly bow,
If you'll only cease your asking,
  Who will care for mother now?

CHORUS.

Soon in Heaven I will join you,
  In that happy, happy land,
Where the saints and angels singing,
  Praise the Lord, that holy land.

When you cross the river Jordan,
  Let not anxious thoughts arise,
I am coming, coming after,
  Angels bear me to the skies.
Let no thoughts of coming sorrow,
  Cloud your placid, peaceful brow,
You can confidently answer,
  God will care for mother now.
        CHORUS.—Soon in Heaven, &c.

Oh! when in death those eyelids close,
  When they bear thee to the tomb,
When life's arduous work is done,
  When your maker calls you home,
And when again to dust you turn,
  When in heaven rise again,
There's where no earthly sorrows come;
  God will guard your mother, then.
        CHORUS.—Soon in Heaven, &c.

YES I WOULD THE WAR WERE OVER.

(Air.—" When this Cruel War is Over.")

Yes I would this war were over,
Would this cruel work were done;
With my country re-united,
And the battles fought and and won.
Let the contest now before us,
Be decided by the sword;
For the war cannot be ended,
Till the Union is restored.

CHORUS—Yes I would this war were over,
Would this cruel work were done;
With my country re-united,
And the battles fought and won.

Dead upon the field of battle,
Fathers, sons and brothers lie,
Friends are waiting—wives and mothers,
Looking for them by and by.
Far away from home forever,
Many a noble boy lies slain,
Look not for thy child fond mother,
Thou shalt see him not again.
CHORUS.—Yes I would this war, &c.

Yes I would the war were ended,
And the cruel struggle o'er;
But our flag must be defended,
And the country as before.
Peace indeed is Heaven's blessing,
Though its joys are easy lost;
Still we'll battle for the nation,
Whatso'er it yet may cost.
CHORUS.—Yes I would the war, &c.

TENTING ON THE OLD CAMP GROUND.

We're tenting to-night on the old camp-ground,
  Give us a song to cheer
Our weary hearts, a song of home
  And friends we love so dear!

CHORUS—Many are the hearts that are weary to-night,
      Wishing for the war to cease;
    Many are the hearts looking for the right,
      To see the dawn of peace;
    Tenting to-night, tenting to-night,
      Tenting on the old camp-ground.

We've been tenting to-night on the old camp-ground,
  Thinking of the days gone by;
Of the loved ones at home, that gave us the hand,
  And the tear that said: Good-bye!
    CHORUS.—Many are the hearts, &c.

We are tired of war on the old camp-ground;
  Many are dead and gone,
Of the brave and true, who've left their homes;
  Others have been wounded long.
    CHORUS.—Many are the hearts, &c.

We've been fighting to-day on the old camp-ground;
  Many are lying near,
Some are dead, and some are dying,
  Many are in tears!

CHORUS—Many are the hearts that are weary to-night,
      Wishing for the war to cease;
    Many are the hearts looking for the right,
      To see the dawn of peace;
    Dying to-night, dying to-night,
      Dying on the old camp-ground.

I'VE COME HOME TO DIE.

Dear mother, I remember well
  The parting kiss you gave to me,
When merry rang the village bell,
  My heart was full of joy and glee.
I did not deem that one short year,
  Would crush the hopes that soared so high;
Oh! mother dear, draw near to me,
  Dear mother, I've come home to die.

CHORUS.

Call sister, brother, to my side,
    And take your soldier's last good-bye;
  Oh! mother, dear, draw near to me,
    Dear mother, I've come home to die.

Hark! mother, 'tis the village bell,
  I can no longer with you stay;
My country calls to arms! to arms!
  The foe advances in fierce array!
The vision's past, I feel that now,
  For my country I can only sigh;
Oh! mother, dear, draw near to me,
  Dear mother, I've come home to die.

CHORUS.—Call sister, &c.

Dear mother, sister, brother, all,
  One parting kiss—to all good-bye;
Weep not, but clasp your hands in mine,
  And let me like a soldier die!
I've met the foe upon the field,
  Where kindred fiercely did defy.
I fought for right—God bless our flag!
  Dear mother, I've come home to die.

CHORUS.—Call sister, &c.

GRAFTED INTO THE ARMY.

Our Jimmy has gone for to live in a tent,
  They have grafted him into the army;
He finally puckered up courage and went,
  When they grafted him into the army.
I told them the child was too young: alas!
  At the Captain's fore quarters, they say, he would pass,
They train'd him up well in the infantry class—
  So they grafted him into the army.

CHORUS—O Jimmy, farewell! your brothers fell
      Way down in Alabarmy;
    I thought they would spare a lone widder's heir,
      But they grafted him into the army.

Dressed up in his unicorn, dear little chap!
  They have grafted him into the army;
It seems but a day since he sot in my lap;
  But they grafted him into the army;
And these are the trousers, he used to wear—
  The very same buttons—the patch and the tear—
But Uncle Sam gave him a bran new pair,
  When they grafted him into the army.
              CHORUS.—O, Jimmy, farewell! &c.

Now, in my provisions I see him revealed,
  They have grafted him into the army;
A picket beside the contented field,
  They have grafted him into the army.
He looks kinder sickish—begins to cry,
  A big volunteer standing right in his eye!
Oh! what if the ducky should up and die,
  Now they've grafted him into the army.
              CHORUS.—O, Jimmy, farewell! &c.

MOTHER IS THE BATTLE OVER.

Mother is the battle over?
Thousands have been slain, they say,
Is my father coming? Tell me,
Have the patriots gain'd the day?
Is he well, or is he wounded—
Mother, do you think he's slain?
If you know I pray you tell me,
Will my father come again?

Mother dear, you're always sighing,
Since you last the papers read,
Tell me now why you are crying,
Why that cap is on your head?
Oh! I see you can not tell me—
Father's one among the slain,
Although he loved us very dearly,
He will never come again.

Yes, my boy, your noble father,
Is one number'd with the slain—
We shall not see him more on earth,
But in heaven we'll meet again.
He died for America's glory,
Our day may not be far between,
But I hope at the last moment,
That we shall all meet again.

ELLSWORTH'S AVENGERS.

Air.—"Annie Lisle."

Down where the patriot army,
　Near Potomac's side;
Guards the glorious cause of freedom,
　Gallant Ellsworth died.
Brave was the noble chieftain;
　At his country's call,
Hastened to the field of battle,
　And was first to fall!

CHORUS—Strike, freemen, for the Union!
　　　Sheath your swords no more;
　　　While remains in arms a traitor,
　　　On Columbia's shore!

Entering the traitor city,
　With his soldiers true;
Leading up the Zouave columns,
　Fixed became his view.
See: that rebel flag is floating
　O'er yon building tall;
Spoke he, while his dark eye glistened,
　Boys, that flag must fall!

　　　　CHORUS.—Strike, freemen, &c.

Quickly, from its proud position,
　That base flag was torn;
Trampled 'neath the feet of freemen,
　Circling Ellsworth's form.
See him bear it down the landing,
　Past the traitor's door;
Hear him groan: Oh! God, they've shot him!
　Ellsworth is no more.

CHORUS.—Strike, freemen, &c.

First to fall, thou youthful martyr,
    Hapless was thy fate;
Hastened we, as thy avengers,
    From thy native State.
Speed we on, from town and city,
    Not for wealth or fame;
But because we love the Union,
    And our Ellsworth's name.
                CHORUS.—Strike, freemen, &c.

Traitors' hands shall never sunder
    That for which you died;
Hear the oath our lips now utter,
    Thou, our nation's pride.
By our hopes of yon bright heaven!
    By the land we love!
By the God who reigns above us!
    We'll avenge thy blood.
                CHORUS.—Strike, freemen. &c.

A WELCOME TO THE SOLDIERS.

We come, brave defenders of freedom, we come,
To welcome you, welcome you, welcome you home;
We parted in sadness, with anguish and fears,
But we welcome you gladly, 'mid smiling and tears.

Our smiles of the warmest and fondest we give,
To heroes returned, to the soldiers who live;
But tears of deep sorrow we shed o'er the urn
Of the brave ones, the loved ones, who never return.

They went from us nobly, the right to maintain,
We weep when we see that they come not again;
But freedom must triumph, whatever the cost,
And the blood of the hero can never be lost.

We yield our heart's honor to them and to you,
Our country's defenders, the brave and the true;
With thanks and with blessings, to greet you we come,
And welcome you, welcome you, welcome you home.

WHEN THIS CRUEL WAR IS OVER.

WORDS AND MUSIC BY HENRY TUCKER.

Dearest love, do you remember
    When we last did meet,
How you told me that you loved me,
    Kneeling at my feet?
Oh! how proud you stood before me,
    In your suit of blue,
When you vow'd to me and country,
    Ever to be true.

CHORUS—Weeping, sad and lonely,
    Hopes and fear, how vain;
    Yet praying, when this cruel war is over,
    Praying: that we meet again!

When the summer breeze is sighing,
    Mournfully, along!
Or when autumn leaves are falling,
    Sadly breathes the song.
Oft, in dreams, I see thee lying
    On the battle plain,
Lonely, wounded, even dying,
    Calling, but in vain.

        CHORUS.—Weeping, sad and lonely, &c.

If, amid the din of battle,
    Nobly you should fall,
Far away from those who love you,
    None to hear you call;
Who would whisper words of comfort,
    Who would soothe your pain?
Ah! the many cruel fancies,
    Ever in my brain.

        CHORUS.—Weeping, sad and lonely, &c.

But o r country called you, darling,
    Angels cheer your way;
While our nation's sons are fighting,
    We can only pray.
Nobly strike for God and liberty,
    Let all nations see
How we love our starry banner,
    Emblem of the free!

        CHORUS.—Weeping, sad and lonely, &c.

GLORY HALLELUJAH! No. 1.

John Brown's body lies mouldering in the grave,
John Brown's body lies slumbering in the grave,
But John Brown's soul is marching with the brave,
      His soul is marching on.

CHORUS.
     Glory, glory, hallelujah,
     Glory, glory, hallelujah,
     Glory, glory, hallelujah,
     His soul is marching on.

He has gone to be a soldier in the army of the Lord,
He is sworn as a private in the ranks of the Lord,
He shall stand at Armageddon with his brave old sword,
      When heaven is marching on
         CHORUS.—Glory, &c.

He shall file in front when the lines of battle form,
He shall face to front when the squares of battle form,
Time with the column and charge with the storm,
      When men are marching on.
         CHORUS.—Glory, &c.

Ah! foul tyrants do you hear him as he comes?
Ah! foul traitors do you know him as he comes,
In the thunder of the cannon and the roll of the drums,
      As we go marching on?
         CHORUS.—Glory, &c.

Men may die and moulder in the dust,
Men may die and arise again from dust,
Shoulder to shoulder in the ranks of the just,
      When God is marching on.
         CHORUS.—Glory, &c.

GLORY HALLELUJ ! No. 2.

John Brown died on a scaffold for the slave;
Dark was the hour when we dug his hallowed grave;
Now God avenges the life he gladly gave—
      Freedom reigns to-day!

   CHORUS—Glory, glory, hallelujah,
      Glory, glory, hallelujah,
      Glory, glory, hallelujah,
      Freedom reigns to-day.

John Brown sowed and his harvesters are we;
Honor to him who has made the bondman free!
Loved evermore shall our noble ruler be—
      Freedom reigns to-day!
      CHORUS.—Glory, &c.

John Brown's body lies mouldering in the grave;
Bright o'er the sod let the starry banner wave,—
Lo! for the millions he periled all to save,
      Freedom reigns to day!
      CHORUS.—Glory, &c.

John Brown lives—we are gaining on our foes—
Right shall be the victor whatever may oppose—
Fresh, through the darkness, the wind of morning blows—
      Freedom reigns to-day!
      CHORUS.—Glory, &c.

John Brown dwells where the battle strife is o'er
Fate cannot harm him nor sorrow stir him more;
Earth will remember the crown of thorns he wore,
      Freedom reigns to-day!
      CHORUS.—Glory, &c.

John Brown's body lies mouldering in the grave;
John Brown lives in the triumphs of the brave;
John Brown's soul not a higher joy can crave—
      Freedom reigns to-day!
      CHORUS.—Glory, &c.

GLORY HALLELUJAH ! No. 3.

John Brown's body lies a mouldering in the grave,   [save,
While weep the sons of bondage, whom he ventured all to
But tho' he lost his life in struggling for the slave,
            His soul is marching on!
CHORUS—Glory, Glory Hallelujah!
            Glory, Glory Hallelujah!
            Glory, Glory Hallelujah!
            His soul is marching on.

John Brown was a hero undaunted, true and brave;   [save;
And Kansas knew his valor, when he fought her rights to
And now, though grass grows green above his grave,
            His soul is marching on.
                        CHORUS.—Glory, &c.

He captured Harper's Ferry with his nineteen men so true,
And he frightened Old Virginny, till she trembled through
      and through,
They hung him for a traitor: themselves a traitor crew;
            But his soul is marching on.
                        CHORUS.—Glory, &c.

John Brown was John the Baptist of Christ we are to see,
Christ who of the bondman shall the Liberator be; [be free;
And soon, throughout the sunny South, the slaves shall all
            For his soul is marching on.
                        CHORUS.—Glory, &c.

The conflict that he heralded, he looks from Heaven to view,
On the army of the Union, with his Flag, red, white and blue,
And Heaven shall ring with anthems o'er the deed they
      mean to do;
            For his soul is marching on.
                        CHORUS.—Glory, &c.

Ye soldiers of Freedom, then strike, while strike you may,
The death-blow of oppression, in a better time and way;
For the dawn of old John Brown has brightened into day,
            And his soul is marching on.
                        CHORUS.—Glory, &c.

GLORY HALLELUJAH ! No. 4.

Glory, Hally, Hallelujah!
Glory, Hally, Hallelujah!
Glory, Hally, Hallelujah!
Hip, hip, hip, hip, Hurrah!

Our Soldiers, now, are marching to'ards the South,
Our Soldiers, now, are marching to'ards the South.
Our Soldiers, now, are marching to'ards the South,
To wipe out Secession.

CHORUS.

Glory! Glory! Hallelujah!
The Stars and Stripes forever wave!
Glory! Glory! Hallelujah!
The Union we shall save!

Treason, soon, will be forced to dig its grave,
Treason, soon, will be forced to dig its grave,
Treason, soon, will be forced to dig its grave,
Never again to rise!

CHORUS.—Glory! Glory! &c.

The Rebels, now, are shaking with alarm,
The Rebels, now, are shaking with alarm,
The Rebels, now, are shaking with alarm,
Want to be let alone!

CHORUS.—Glory! Glory! &c.

Run, Jeff, run! if you wish to save your neck,
Run, Jeff, run! if you wish to save your neck,
Run, Jeff, run! if you wish to save your neck,
For we are on your heels!

CHORUS.—Glory! Glory! &c.

To Friends, hope, but to traitors we'll give rope,
To Friends, hope, but to traitors we'll give rope,
To Friends, hope, but to traitors we'll give rope,
    A warning to mankind!

             CHORUS.—Glory! Glory! &c.

We've whipt them on the plain, whipt 'em on the sea,
We've whipt them on the plain, whipt 'em on the sea,
We've whipt them on the plain, whipt 'em on the sea,
    Victory has been ours!

             CHORUS.—Glory! Glory! &c.

Then, three cheers for our noble Volunteers,
Then, three cheers for our noble Volunteers,
Then, three cheers for our noble Volunteers,
    And gallant Navy Blues!

             CHORUS.—Glory! Glory! &c.

Again our flag will float throughout the land,
Again our flag will float throughout the land,
Again our flag will float throughout the land,
    Triumphant, Proud and Free!

             CHORUS.—Glory! Glory! &c.

United once more, may God keep us so,
United once more, may God keep us so,
United once more, may God keep us so,
    Forever, and for aye!

             CHORUS.—Glory! Glory! &c.

4

GLORY HALLELUJAH! No. 5.

John Brown's body lies a mouldering in the grave,
John Brown's body lies a mouldering in the grave,
John Brown's body lies a mouldering in the grave,
    His soul's marching on!

    CHORUS—Glory, Hally, Hallelujah!
        Glory, Hally, Hallelujah!
        Glory, Hally, Hallelujah!
        His soul's marching on. *

He's gone to be a soldier in the army of our Lord,
He's gone to be a soldier in the army of our Lord,
He's gone to be a soldier in the army of our Lord,
    His soul's marching on!
    CHORUS.—Glory, Hally, Hallelujah! &c.

John Brown's knapsack is strapped upon his back,
John Brown's knapsack is strapped upon his back,
John Brown's knapsack is strapped upon his back,
    His soul's marching on!
    CHORUS.—Glory, Hally, Hallelujah! &c.

His pet lambs will meet him on the way,
His pet lambs will meet him on the way,
His pet lambs will meet him on the way,
    They go marching on!
    CHORUS.—Glory, Hally, Hallelujah! &c.

They will hang Jeff Davis to a sour apple tree,
They will hang Jeff Davis to a sour apple tree,
They will hang Jeff Davis to a sour apple tree,
    As they go marching along!
    CHORUS.—Glory, Hally, Hallelujah! &c.

Now, three rousing cheers for the Union!
Now, three rousing cheers for the Union!
Now, three rousing cheers for the Union!
    As we go marching on!

KISS ME MOTHER, KISS YOUR DARLING.

Words by Letta C. Lord.　　Music by G. F. Root.

Kiss me, mother, kiss your darling,
　Lean my head upon your breast,
Fold your loving arms around me,
　I am weary, let me rest.
Scenes of life are switly fading,
　Brighter seems the other shore;
I am standing by the river,
　Angels wait to waft me o'er.

CHORUS—Kiss me, mother, kiss your darling
　　Lean my head upon your breast,
　　Fold your loving arms around me,
　　I am weary, let me rest.

Kiss me, mother, kiss your darling,
　Breathe a blessing on my brow;
For, I'll soon be with the angels,
　Fainter grows my breath e'en now.
Tell the loved ones not to murmur;
　Say I died our flag to save,
And that I shall slumber sweetly'
　In the soldier's honored grave.
　　　　CHORUS.—Kiss me, mother, &c.

Oh! how dark this world is growing,
　Hark! I hear the angel band,
How I long to join their number
　In that fair and happy land!
Hear you not that heavenly music,
　Floating near so soft and low?
I must leave you—farewell mother!
　Kiss me once before I go.
　　　　CHORUS.—Kiss me, mother, &c.

BUMMERS COME AND MEET US.

(Air—"John Brown's Song.")

Freedom is our leader now, we've had our last retreat,
Freedom is our leader now, we've had our last retreat,
Freedom is our leader now, we've had our last retreat,
    We'll now go marching on.

        Say, brothers, will you meet us?
        Say, brothers, will you meet us?
        Say, brothers, will you meet us?
          As we go marching on.

Thomas turned a *Somerset*, and gave the rebels rats;
Thomas turned a *Somerset*, and gave the rebels rats;
Thomas turned a *Somerset*, and gave the rebels rats;
    And sent them rolling home.

        Oh, brothers, we will join him;
        Oh, brothers, we will join him;
        Oh, brothers, we will join him;
          And send them rolling home.

How are you, Johnny Bull, old boy? How are you, Johnny
    Bull?
How are you, Johnny Bull, old boy? How are you, Johnny
    Bull?   [full,
If you want to fight, old Roast Beef, you will get your belly
    And then go rolling home.

        Oh, Johnny, don't you fight us;
        Oh, Johnny, don't you fight us;
        Oh, Johnny, don't you fight us;
          Or we'll send you rolling home.

We'll have a farm in Dixie, boys, and put some freemen on it;
We'll have a farm in Dixie, boys, and put some freemen on it;
We'll have a farm in Dixie, boys, and put some freemen on it;
    And then we'll simmer down.

Oh, sisters, come and join us;
Oh, sisters, come and join us;
Oh, sisters, come and join us;
    Way down in Dixie's Land.

Oh, boys, we'll sip our cobblers then, and cloud our meer-
    schaum pipes;
Oh, boys, we'll sip our cobblers then, and cloud our meer-
    schaum pipes;
Oh, boys, we'll sip our cobblers then, and cloud our meer-
    schaum pipes;
    Way down in Dixie's land.

Oh, bummers come and meet us,
Oh, bummers come and meet us,
Oh, bummers come and meet us,
    Way down in Dixie's land.

There lies the whisky-bottle empty on the shelf,
There lies the whisky-bottle empty on the shelf,
There lies the whisky-bottle empty on the shelf,
    But there's some more in the Demi-John.

Oh, bummers, don't you leave us,
Oh, bummers, don't you leave us,
Oh, bummers, don't you leave us,
    We'll soon go marching on.

The girls we left behind us, boys, our sweethearts at the
    North,
The girls we left behind us, boys, our sweethearts at the
    North,
The girls we left behind us, boys, our sweethearts at the
    North,
    Smile on us as we march.

Oh, sweethearts, don't forget us,
Oh, sweethearts, don't forget us,
Oh, sweethearts, don't forget us,
    We'll soon come marching home.

MARCHING ALONG. No. 1.

Our Country has called her brave sons to the field;
To false-hearted traitors she never must yield;
Then forward true soldiers, let this be our song;
To conquer or die! we are marching along!

CHORUS.

Marching along, we are marching along,
The Union to save we are marching along!
Let traitors beware! for there's death in our song;
To conquer or die! we are marching along!

Tho' strewn be our path with the dying and dead;
Tho' to battle, through rivers of blood, we are led;
Our hearts will be firm, and our courage be strong;
For God is our guide, as we're marching along!

CHORUS.—Marching along, &c.

Near the graves where our comrades lie sleeping in death,
We soon for our country may yield our last breath;
We'll fight till we die! let our flag but still wave!
For a bright ray of glory will hallow each grave!

CHORUS.—Marching along, &c.

Then, on let us march! boys—on, to the fight!
Success must be ours, since our cause is the right;
Three cheers for our flag, and three cheers for our song
to conquer or die! we are marching along!

CHORUS.—Marching along, &c.

MARCHING ALONG. No. 2.

The army is gathering from near and from far;
The trumpet is sounding the call for the war;
A brave man's our leader, he's gallant and strong,
We'll gird on our armor, and be marching along.

CHORUS.

Marching along, we are marching along,
Gird on the armor and be marching along;
A brave man's our leader, he's gallant and strong;
For God and our country, we're marching along!

The foe is before us, in battle array;
But let us not waver, or turn from the way.
The Lord is our strength, and the Union's our song;
With courage and faith, we are marching along.

CHORUS.—Marching along, &c.

We sigh for our country, we mourn for our dead;
For them, now, we hope the last blood has been shed;
Our cause is the right one: our foe's in the wrong;
Then gladly we'll sing as we're marching along!

CHORUS.—Marching along, &c.

Our wives and our children we leave in your care;
We know you will help them their sorrows to bear;
'Tis hard thus to part, but we hope 'twon't be long;
We'll keep up our hearts as we're marching along!

CHORUS.—Marching along, &c.

The flag of our country is floating on high;
We'll stand by that Flag, till we conquer or die!
A brave man's our leader, he's gallant and strong;
We'll gird on our armor, and be marching along!

CHORUS.—Marching along, &c.

MY MARYLAND.

BY STONE-WALL JACKSON.

My barefoot bands are on thy shore,
  Maryland! Maryland!
Their touch is on thy temple-door,
  Maryland! Maryland!
Fling open every dry goods store,
Bring boots and shoes out by the score,
Forth every whisky barrel pour,
  Maryland, my Maryland!

Hark to a wandering son's appeal,
  Maryland! Maryland!
My glorious State, to thee I kneel,
  Maryland! Maryland!
Give us potatoes, bread, cornmeal;
Thy peerless chivalry reveal,
And gird our beauteous limbs with *steal*,
  Maryland, my Maryland!

Thou wilt not cower in the dust,
  Maryland! Maryland!
Thy burning sword shall never rust,
  Maryland! Maryland!
Take, take these notes of mine on trust,
Confederate bonds may not be just
The things you want—but then you must,
  Maryland, my Maryland!

Come! with thy *pan*-oplied array,
  Maryland! Maryland!
Come! with thy stacks of grain and hay,
  Maryland! Maryland!
We've famished long upon the way,
Our steeds have starved this many a day,
Come! give us what we want, I say,
  Maryland, my Maryland!

Come! for thy red-eye's good and strong,
    Maryland! Maryland!
Thy hesitation does thee wrong,
    Maryland! Maryland!
Come to thy own heroic throng!
We've brought some little ills along,
That wouldn't do to sing in song,
    Maryland, my Maryland!

I see the blush upon thy cheek,
    Maryland! Maryland!
But thou was always rather weak,
    Maryland! Maryland!
But lo! there surges forth a shriek,
Potomac calls to Chesapeake;
I guess from out thine arms I'll streak,
    Maryland, my Maryland!

Thou wilt not yield the Southern toll,
    Maryland! Maryland!
Thou wilt not crouch to Jeff's control,
    Maryland! Maryland!
Better the fire upon thee roll,
Better the shot, the blade, the bowl—
I think so, too, upon my soul!
    Maryland, my Maryland!

I hear the distant thunder hum,
    Maryland! Maryland!
Old Lincoln's bugle, fife and drum—
    Maryland! Maryland!
I'm not exactly deaf and dumb—
I know the sounds of shell and bomb—
Farewell! again I'll never come,
Since you don't welcome Southern scum—
    Maryland, my Maryland!

"OUR" MARYLAND.

The rebel thieves were sure of thee,
    Maryland, our Maryland!
And boasted they would welcome be,
    Maryland, our Maryland!
But now they turn and now they flee,
With Stone-wall Jackson and with Lee,
And loyal souls once more are free!
    Maryland, our Maryland!

With plundered guns and stolen swords,
    Maryland, our Maryland!
On thee they came in ruffian hordes,
    Maryland, our Maryland!
With raving oaths and roaring words,
And pirate's knives and hangman's cords,
They swarmed across the border fords,
    Maryland, our Maryland!

Through passways of the mountain crags,
    Maryland, our Maryland!
They bore their vile secession flags,
    Maryland, our Maryland!
Like beggar troops in filthy rags,
Barefooted men, and spavined nags,
Their voices hoarse with Southern brags,
    Maryland, our Maryland!

Like dogs all raving for a crumb,
    Maryland, our Maryland!
They madly rushed for bread and rum,
    Maryland, our Maryland!
But backward run, with voices dumb,
And drooping hands and faces glum,
They ran from Union's rolling drum,
    Maryland, our Maryland!

COMRADES I AM DYING.

Comrades, comrades, I am dying!
See the crimson fountain flow!
Sick and wounded, I am dying,
On the field among the foe.
But the angels hover round me,
They will guard me when I sleep,
Comrades, onward to the battle,
Do not for a soldier weep.

CHORUS—Comrades, comrades, I am dying!
See the crimson fountain flow!
Sick and wounded, I am dying,
On the field among the foe.

Comrades, comrades, I am dying!
For I see my mother now,
See her coming down from heaven
With a wreath upon her brow.
God has sent her to the soldier,
She will teach him how to die;
And when He hath called my spirit,
She will bear it to the sky.
CHORUS.—Comrades, comrades, &c.

Comrades, comrades, I am dying!
Soon I'll be among the blest,
Fare—Oh! fare you well, forever,
I am going there to rest.
For my mother's arms entwine me,
And I can no longer stay;
Onward comrades, to the battle,
Angels they will lead the way.
CHORUS.—Comrades, comrades, &c.

OUR COLOR GUARD.

BATTLE SONG AND CHORUS.

Words by Thomas H. Diehl.   Mus c by Henry Tucker.

Now onward! onward! let it wave,
 Amid the cannon's roar,
Borne by the noble and the brave,
 Thro' streams of crimson gore;
Amid the battle's fiercest strife,
 There ever let it be,
And guard it with devoted life,
 That standard of the free!

CHORUS—Hurrah, boys! Hurrah, boys!
  Hurrah! Hurrah! Hurrah!
 Onward! onward ever be
 "Our color guard" supplied.

"Stand by those colors!" many an eye
 Is looking up to-day,
To see that glorious emblem fly
 Where danger checks the way.
"Stand by those colors!" many a soul
 Will gain new strength to die,
If in the red tide's fiercest roll
 Those colors proudly fly.
  CHORUS.—Hurrah, boys! &c.

On! color guard! Oh, noble, brave,
 How one by one they fall,
But not their fate! nor yet the grave
 Our brave lads can appall.
Now from the ranks lean eagerly,
 Like groom to meet his bride
A score of volunteers—and see!
 "Our color guard" supplied.
  CHORUS.—Hurrah, boys! &c.

THE OLD UNION WAGON.

BY ROBERT M. HART.

(*Air.—"Wait for the Wagon."*)

The eagle of Columbia, in majesty and pride,
Still soars aloft in glory, though traitors have defied
The flag we dearly cherish—the emblem of our will—
Baptised in blood of heroes 'way down on Bunker Hill.

CHORUS.—Sam built the wagon,
The Old Union Wagon,
The star-crested wagon,
To give the boys a ride.

The war screech of that eagle is heard from shore to shore,
For clouds of dark rebellion our sky has shrouded o'er;
But freedom and its sunlight will break the gloomy pall,
And scorch the brow of treason with powder, shell and ball.

Bring on the wagon,
The Old Union Wagon,
The tri-colored wagon,
We're waiting for a ride.

King Cotton may be master o'er those who bend the knee,
But cannot rule a people who ever will be free,
As are the winds of heaven—whose every thought and deed,
Shall emanate from Justice, and not from Cotton seed.

Stick to the wagon,
The Old Union Wagon,
The triumphal wagon,
And we'll all safely ride.

Old Abe is in the wagon, and Scott is by his side,
And Seward drives the horses to take a Union ride;
While Butler is not idle, and Cameron is true,
And we're all in the wagon with Yankee doodle-doo.

Shove on the wagon,
The Old Union Wagon,
God bless the wagon,
While patriots shall ride.

There's none can smash the wagon—'tis patented and strong,
And built of pure devotion, by those who hate the wrong—
Its wheels are made of freedom, which patriots adore:
The spokes, when rightly counted, just number thirty-four.

Keep in the wagon,
The Old Union Wagon,
The oft-tested wagon,
While millions take a ride.

A BOLD BRAVE CREW—SONG OF THE SEA.

A bold, brave crew and an ocean blue,
And a ship that loves the blast;
With a good wind piping merrily
In the tall and gallant mast.

CHORUS—Ha! Ha! my boys,
These are the joys,
Of the noble and brave;
Who love a life
In the tempest's strife,
And a home on the mountain wave.

When driving rain of the hurricane
Puts the light of the light-house out,
And the growing thunder sounds its gong
On the whirlwind's battle rout.

Ha! Ha! do you think
That the valiant shrink?
No! No! we are bold and brave
And we love to fight,
In the wild midnight,
With the storm on the mountain wave!

Breezes that die where the green woods sigh,
To the landsman sweet may be,
But give to the brave the broad-backed wave,
And the tempest's midnight glee!

Ha! Ha! the blast,
And the rocking mast,
And the sea wind brisk and cold,
And the thunder's jar,
On the seas afar,
Are the things that suit the bold.

The timbers creak, the sea birds shriek:
There's lightning in yon blast!
Hard to the leeward! mariners,
For the storm is gathering fast!

Ha! Ha! to-night,
Boys, we must fight;
But the winds which o'er us yell,
Shall never scare
The mariner,
In his winged citadel!

ONE AT HOME WHO PRAYS FOR ME,
OR,
WHO HAS NOT A PRAYING MOTHER?

Words by HENRY M. HUNT.   Music by HENRY TUCKER.

At midnight, on my lonely beat,
  When shadow wraps the wood and lea,
A vision seems my view to greet,
  Of one at home who prays for me;
No roses bloom upon her cheek,
  Her form is not a lover's dream,
But o'er that brow so pure and meek,
  A thousand holier beauties gleam.

CHORUS—Who has not a praying mother,
  Wheresoe'er his lot may be!
Ev'ry wand'rer feels in darkest hour,
  There's one at home who prays for me.

How softly shines her silver hair,
  A patient smile is on her face,
And that mild lustrous light of prayer,
  Around her sheds a moonlike grace;
She prays for me so far away—
  The soldier in his holy fight,
And begs that heaven in mercy may
  Protect her boy and bless the right!
              CHORUS.—Who has not, &c.

Still though the leagues lie far between,
  This silent incense of her heart
Steals o'er my soul with breath serene,
  And we no longer are apart;
So guarding thus my lonely beat
  By shadowy wood and haunted lea,
That vision seems my view to greet
  Of her at home who prays for me.
              CHORUS.—Who has not, &c.

WHO WILL CARE FOR MICKY NOW?

A PARODY ON "WHO WILL CARE FOR MOTHER NOW?"

Among the many heroic fellows who drew a prize in the U. S. lottery, was a distinguished Frenchman—from Limerick—the only support of himself. On being told by the Surgeon he would " Pass," he placed his hand on his empty stomach, and while a big tear of bravery rolled down his cheek, exclaimed in accents that would have touched the heart of a wheel-barrow : "Who will care for Micky now?"

Arrah! Molly darlin' I'm drafted,
   Sure I must for a soger go;
An' lave you all alone behind me,
   For to fight the rebel foe—
But, be the powers! me pluck is failin'
   Big drops of swate roll down my brow;
Och, millia murther! I am drafted,
   Who will care for Micky now?

CHORUS—Soon 'gainst ribels I'll be marching,
     Wid the swate upon me brow—
    Och, blud an' nouns! I'm kilt entirely:
     Who will care for Micky now?

Arrah! who will comfort me in sorrow,
   Wi h a drop of gin or beer;
Wash me dirty shirts and stockin's?
   Faix! there's no one I fear—
Me feet are blistered wid the marching,
   Me knapsack makes me shoulders bow—
Pork and crackers are me rations:
   Who will care for Micky now?

      CHORUS.—Soon 'gainst ribels, &c.

Indade I miss me feather pillow
   An' bed on which I used to lie—
The pine planks make me feel uneasy,
   If I had wings, och! wudn't I fly!
But one ov me legs is stiff, dear,
   Since I was kicked be Murphy's cow;
I'm afraid I niver can skedaddle:
   Who will care for Micky now?

      CHORUS.—Soon 'gainst ribels, &c.

LIFE ON THE OCEAN WAVE.

A life on the ocean wave,
  A home on the rolling deep,
Where the scattered waters rave,
  And the winds their revels keep.
Like an eagle caged I pine,
  On this dull unchanging shore;
Oh, give me the splashing brine,
  The spray and the tempest's roar.

CHORUS.—A life, &c.

Once more on the deck I stand,
  Of my own swift gliding, craft,
Set sail, farewell to the land!—
  The gale flows fair abaft.
We shoot through the sparkling foam
  Like an ocean bird set free—
Like the ocean bird our home,
  We'll find far out in the sea.

CHORUS.—A life, &c.

The land is no longer in view,
  The clouds have begun to frown,
But with a stout vessel and crew,
  We'll say, let the storm come down.
And the song of our hearts shall be,
  While the winds and the waters rave,
A life on the heaving sea,
  A home on the bounding wave!

CHORUS.—A life, &c.

WE ARE COMING FATHER ABRAHAM.

We are coming, Father Abraham,
   Three hundred thousand more;
From Mississippi's winding stream,
   And from New England's shore.
We leave our ploughs and workshops,
   Our wives and children dear;
With hearts too full of utterance,
   With but a silent tear.
We dare not look behind us,
   But steadfastly before—
We are coming Father Abraham,
   Three hundred thousand more!

CHORUS.

We are coming, we are coming,
   Our Union to restore;
We are coming, Father Abraham,
   With three hundred thousand more.

If you look across the hill-tops,
   That meet the Northern sky;
Long moving lines of rising dust,
   Your vision may descry.
And now the wind, an instant,
   Tears the cloudy veil aside;
And floats aloft our spangled flag,
   In glory and in pride.
And bayonets in the sunlight gleam,
   And bands brave music pour—
We are coming, Father Abraham,
   Three hundred thusand more.

       CHORUS.—We are coming, &c.

If you look all up our valleys,
  Where the growing harvests shine;
You may see our sturdy farmer boys,
  Fast forming into line.
And children from their mother's knees,
  Are pulling at the weeds;
And learning how to reap and sow,
  Against their country's needs.
And a farewell group stands weeping
  At every cottage door—
We are coming Father Abraham,
  Three hundred thousand more!

CHORUS.—We are coming, &c.

You have called us, and we're coming,
  By Richmond's bloody tide;
To lay us down for freedom's sake,
  Our brothers' bones beside;
Or from foul treason's savage group
  To wrench the murderous blade;
And in the face of foreign foes,
  Its fragments to parade.
Six hundred thousand loyal men,
  And true, have gone before—
We are coming, Father Abraham,
  Three hundred thousand more!

CHORUS.—We are coming, &c.

HAIL! OUR COUNTRY'S NATAL MORN.

Hail our country's natal morn!
Hail our spreading kindred born!
Hail thou banner not yet torn!
   Still waving o'er the Free!
While this day, in festal throng,
Millions swell the patriot song,
Shall not we thy notes prolong?
   Hallowed Jubilee!

CHORUS—Hail! our country's natal morn,
   Hail! ye millions yet unborn,
   Hail! thou banner not yet torn,
      Still waving o'er the free.
   While this day, in festal throng,
   Millions swell the patriot song,
   Shall not we thy notes prolong,
      Hallowed jubilee?

Who would sever Freedom's shrine?
Who would draw th' invidious line?
Though by birth one spot be mine,
   Yet dear is all the rest—
Dear to me the South's fair land,
Dear the central mountain band,
Dear New England's rocky strand,
   Dear the prairied West.
        CHORUS.—Hail! our country's, &c.

By our altars pure and free,
By our law's deep-rooted tree,
By the past dread memory,
   And by our martyr's name:
By our common parent tongue,
By our hopes, bright, buoyant, young,
By the tie of country strong,
   United we'll remain.

CHORUS.—Hail! our country's, &c.

Brothers! have ye bled in vain?
Ages! must ye droop again?
Maker! shall we rashly stain
    These blessings sent by thee?
No! receive our solemn vow,
While before Thy throne we bow,
Ever to maintain as now,
    "UNION—LIBERTY."

CHORUS.—Hail! our country's, &c.

UNCLE NED.

I once knew a darkey, and his name was Uncle Ned,
    Oh, he died long ago—long ago;
He had no hair on the top of his head,
    The place where the wool ought to grow.

CHORUS.
Lay down the shovel and the hoe,
Hang up the fiddle and the bow;
For no more work for poor old Ned,
He's gone where the good darkies go.

His fingers were long, like the cane in the brake,
    And he had no eyes for to see;
He had no teeth for to eat de hoe cake,
    So he had to let the hoe cake be.

One cold frosty morning old Ned died,
    Oh, the tears down Massa's face run like rain.
For he knew when Ned was laid in the ground
    He'd nebber see his like again.

COLUMBIA, THE GEM OF, &c.

KEY OF G.

O, Columbia! the gem of the ocean.
The home of the brave and the free,
The shrine of each patriot's devotion,
A world offers homage to thee!
Thy mandates make heroes assemble,
When Liberty's form stands in view,—
Thy banners make tyranny tremble,
When borne by the Red, White, and Blue.

CHORUS—When borne by the Red, White and Blue,
When borne by the Red, White and Blue,
Thy banners make .yranny tremble,
When borne by the Red, White and Blue.

When war winged its wide desolation,
And threatened the land to deform,
The ark, then of Freedom's foundation,
Columbia, rode safe through the storm;
With her garlands of vict'ry around her,
When so proudly she bore her brave crew,
With her flag proudly floating before her,
The boast of the Red, White and Blue.

CHORUS.—The boast of the Red, &c.

The wine-cup, the wine-cup bring hither,
And fill you it true to the brim!
May the wreaths they have won never wither,
Nor the stars of their glory grow dim!
May the service united ne'er sever,
But they to their colors prove true!
The Army and Navy forever!
Three cheers for the Red, White and Blue.

OLD DOG TRAY.

The morning meal is past—the next is coming fast—
'Twill bring me a bill that I know I cannot pay,
For meats, both fat and lean, that I was jolly green
To trust beside that old dog Tray.

CHORUS.

Old dog Tray! always hungry—
Meat cannot drive him away;   [kind,
With his tail "druv" in behind, neither gentle nor yet
Is that hungry dog, that old dog Tray.

I hurried home one night, with a rousing appetite,
For nothing had I tasted the whole of that long day.
But Oh! how I was done—not a thing was left but bone—
All eaten by that old dog Tray.

CHORUS.—Old dog Tray, &c.

The stakes I thought my own, had vanished one by one,
Those cutlets, those chops too, had all passed away;
Those tenderloins were gone—they each and all had flown—
Stolen by that old dog Tray.

CHORUS.—Old dog Tray, &c.

With naught to break my fast, my eyes on Tray I cast,
Who looked as though he felt what my breaking heart
would say;
But oh! 'twas all deceit—twas *he* who stole my meat,
That hungry dog, that old dog Tray.

CHORUS.—Old dog Tray, &c.

DO THEY MISS ME AT HOME.

Do they miss me at home, do they miss me!
  'Twould be an assurance most dear,
To know that this moment some loved one,
  Were saying I wish he was here,
To feel that the group at the fireside
  Were thinking of me as I roam,
Oh, yes, 'twould be joy beyond measure,
  To know that they miss'd me at home,
  To know that they miss'd me at home.

When twilight approaches, the season
  That ever is sacred to song,
Does some one repeat my name over,
  And sigh that I tarry so long?
And is there a chord in the music
  That's missed when my voice is away,
And a chord in each heart that awaketh
  Regret at my wearisome stay,
  Regret at my wearisome stay.

Do they sit me a chair near the table,
  When evening's home pleasures are nigh,
When the candles are lit in the parlor,
  And the stars in the calm azure sky?
And when the " good-nights " are repeated,
  And all lay them down to their sleep,
Do they think of the absent, and waft me
  A whispered "good-night " while they weep,
  A whispered "good-night " while they weep?

Do they miss me at home—do they miss me
  At morning, at noon, or at night?
And lingers one gloomy shade round them
  That only my presence can light?
Are joys less invitingly welcome,
  And pleasures less hale than before,
Because one is missed from the circle,
  Because I am with them no more,
  Because I am with them no more!

WE MISS THEE AT HOME.

We miss thee at home, yes, we miss thee,
  Since the hour we bade the adieu;
And prayers have encircled thy pathway,
  From anxious hearts, loving and true,
That the Saviour would guide and protect thee,
  As far from the loved ones you roam,
And whisper whene'er thou wert saddened,
  "They miss thee, all miss thee at home."

When morning awakes us from slumber,
  We catch from the lips the first kiss,
And fold in a wandering zephyr,
  To be wafted to him whom we miss;
And when we have joined the "home circle,"
  And replaced the still vacant chair,
In each eye rose the gathering tear-drop,
  For him we were wont to see there.

The shadows of evening are falling—
  Oh, where is the wanderer now?
The breeze that floats lightly around me,
  Perchance may soon visit his b ow;
Oh, bear on thy bosom a message,
  We are watching, oh, why wilt thou roam?
The heart has grown sad and dejected,
  For we miss thee, all miss thee at home,

UNFURL THE GLORIOUS BANNER.

Unfurl the glorious banner, let it sway upon the breeze,
The emblem of our country's pride, on land, and on the
    seas,
The emblem of our liberty, borne proudly in the wars,
The hope of every freeman, the gleaming stripes and stars.

CHORUS.

Then unfurl the glorious banner out upon the welcoming
    air,
Read the record of the olden time upon its radiance there;
In the battle it shall lead us, and our banner ever be,
A beacon light to glory, and a guide to victory.

The glorious band of patriots who gave the flag its birth,
Have writ with steel in history, the record of its worth;
From east to west, from sea to sea, from pole to tropic sun,
Will eyes grow bright, and hearts throb high at the name
    of Washington.
    CHORUS.—Then unfurl the glorious banner, &c.

Ah! proudly should we bear it, and guard this flag of ours,
Borne bravely in its infancy amidst the darker hours;
Only the brave may bear it, a guardian it shall be,
For those who well have won the right to boast of liberty.
    CHORUS.—Then unfurl the glorious banner, &c.

The meteor flag of seventy-six, long may it wave in pride,
To tell the world how nobly the patriot father's died;
When from the shadows of their night outburst the bril-
    liant sun,
It bathed in light the stripes and stars, and lo! the field
    was won.
    CHORUS.—Then unfurl the glorious banner &c.

TELL MOTHER I DIE HAPPY.

I am dying, comrades, dying,
  As you bear me, lightly tread;
Soon, ah, soon, I shall be lying
  With the silent, sleeping dead!
I am dying, comrades, dying,
  Still the battle rages near;
Tell me, are our foes a flying?
  I die happy, Mother dear!

Chorus—Tell my Mother I die happy,
  That for me she must not weep;
Tell her how I long to kiss her,
  Ere I sunk in death to sleep!

I am going, comrades, going;
  See how damp my forehead's now;
Oh, I see the Angels coming,
  With bright garlands for my brow,
Bear this message to my Mother:
  How in death that God was near,
He to bless and to support me;
  I die happy, Mother dear!

Chorus.—Tell my Mother, &c.

Lay me, comrades, 'neath the willow,
  That grows on the distant shore;
Wrap the Starry Flag around me,
  I would press its folds once more;
Let the cold earth be my pillow,
  And the Stars and Stripes my shroud;
Soon, oh! soon, I shall be marching
  Amid the Heavenly Crowd!

Chorus.—Tell my Mother, &c.

THE LIFE OF A SOLDIER.

Air.—"Tramp, Tramp."

My name is Paddy Doyle,
I'm a native of the soil
Where the purty little shamrock, lively grows;
For a soldier I did list,
Got the bounty in my fist,
A bounty and the nobby suit of clothes.

Chorus—Tramp, tramp, tramp, the boys are marching,
   Cheer up, comrades, let's be gay; [glass,
We will toast each blooming lass, in a full and flowing
With the merry fife and drum we'll march away.

Every pretty girl I mark.
And sometimes I have a lark,
I praise their figure and their beauty;
While the children run and play,
We pass the time away,
Oh! that's what I call doing soger's duty.
    Chorus.—Tramp, tramp, &c.

Whene'er we leave a town,
The damsels pout and frown,
To think that they'll not see us any more;
But I always bear in mind,
The girls I leave behind,
The darling little creatures I adore.
    Chorus.—Tramp, tramp, &c.

Hark! I hear my comrades come,
There's the merry fife and drum,
The sound fills my heart so full of joy;
-Then raise a hearty cheer,
For home and friends so dear,
And success attend the jovial soger boy
    Chorus.—Tramp, tramp, &c.

THE OCTOROON; OR, GLORY, GLORY.

Near the old plantation, at the close o' day,
  Stood a weary mother and her child;
List'ning to the sounds along the valley way,
  While their hearts with hope were throbbing wild.

CHORUS.

Glory, glory how the freedmen sang,
Glory, glory how the old woods rang;
'Twas the loyal army sweeping to the sea,
Flinging out the banner of t e free.

Fly my precious darling to the Union camp,
  I will keep the hounds and hunters here;
Go right through the forest, though it be dark and damp,
  God will keep you, dear one, never fear.

CHORUS.—Glory, &c.

When the blazing camp fire gleamed amid the wood,
  And the boys were halting for the night;
In her wond'rous beauty, little Rosa stood,
  Trembling and alone before their sight.

CHORUS.—Glory, &c.

Then the brave old gunner took her in his arms,
  Thinking of his own dear ones at home;
And through all the marches and the rude alarms,
  Safely brought the little Octoroon.

CHORUS.—Glory, &c.

WILLIE HAS GONE TO THE WAR.

The blue bird is singing its lay,
  To all the sweet flowers of the dale;
The wild bee is roaming, at play;
  And soft is the sigh of the gale;
I stray by the brook-side, alone,
  Where oft we have wandered before,
And weep for my loved one—my own:
  My Willie has gone to the war.

Chorus—Willie has gone to the war, Willie—
  Willie, my loved one—my own:
Willie has gone to the war, Willie—
  Willie, my loved one, has gone.

It was there, where the lily-bells grow,
  That I last saw his noble young face;
But now he has gone to the foe—
  Oh! dearly I love the old place!
The whispering waters repeat
  The name that I love, o'er and o'er,
And daisies, that nod at my feet,
  Say: Willie has gone to the war!

          Chorus.—Willie has gone, &c.

The leaves of the forest will fade,
  The roses will wither and die,
And Spring to our home in the glade,
  On fairy-like pinions, will fly;
But still I will hopefully wait,
  Till the day when those battles are o'er;
And pine like a bird for its mate,
  Till Willie comes home from the war.

          Chorus.—Willie has gone, &c.

GOD WILL CARE FOR MOTHER NOW.

(*Air.—"Who Will Care for Mother Now"?*)

Weep no more, O nobly fallen!
  Banish sorrow from thy heart;
Hark! the angels, round thee hov'ring,
  Words of peace and joy impart.
See they bid you join their number,
  Wreath bright laurels round thy brow,
Murm'ring softly as they crown thee:
  God will care for mother now.

CHORUS—Weep no more, O nobly fallen!
    Let not sorrow cloud thy brow;
    Holy angels round thee whisper:
    God will care for mother now.

When that mother, sad and lonely,
  Mourns her loved and cherished one,
When in agony she murmurs:
  Give me back my darling son!
When she's crushed and bowed with trouble,
  And her heart is filled with fears;
Then, the angels sweetly whisper:
  God will wipe away her tears.
              CHORUS.—Weep no more, &c.

Oh! how sweet those words of comfort
  To the dying soldier's ear!
Who so anxiously is asking:
  "Who will cherish mother here,
When I reach that land of glory,
  And before my Maker bow?"
Sweetly comes the whispered answer:
  God will care for mother now.
              CHORUS.—Weep no more, &c.

BROTHER'S FAINTING AT THE DOOR.

Yonder comes a weary soldier,
  With faltering steps across the moor;
    Mem'ries of the past steal o'er me:
  He totters to the cottage door.
Look! my heart can not deceive me:
  'Tis one we deemed on earth no more,
Call Mother, haste, do not tarry,
  For, brother's fainting at the door.

Chorus—Kindly greet the weary soldier,
    Words of comfort may restore,
  You may have an absent brother,
    Fainting at a stranger's door.

Tell us, brother, of the battle,
  Why you were numbered with the slain;
We, who thought you lost forever,
  Now clasp you to our arms again;
Oh! may others share the blessing,
  Which Heaven kindly keeps in store;
May they meet their absent loved ones,
  Ay, e'en though fainting at the door!

                    Chorus.—Kindly greet, &c.

I was wounded and a pris'ner,
  Our ranks were broken, forced to fly,
Thrown within a gloomy dungeon,
  Away from friends alone to die.
Still the hope was strong within me,
  A cherished hope that would restore:
I have lived by Heaven's blessing,
  To meet my loved ones at the door.

                    Chorus.—Kindly greet, &c.

THE SOLDIER'S FUNERAL.

(*Air.*—"*Ellsworth.*")

Hark! to the shrill trumpet calling,
   It pierces the soft summer air;
Tears from each comrade are falling,
   For the widow and orphan are there;
Bayonets earthward are turning,
   The drum muffled voice breathes around,
Yet he heeds not the voice of the mourner,
   Nor wakes to the soft bugle's sound.

Sleep, soldier, tho' many may mourn thee,
   And weep o'er thy cold form to-day;
Soon, soon will thy kindred forget thee,
   Thy name from the earth pass away;
The man thou hast loved as a brother,
   Some friend in thy place shall have gain'd;
Thy dog shall keep watch for another,
   Thy steed by another be reined.

Tho' many now mourn for thee sadly,
   Soon joyous as ever they'll be;
Thy bright orphan boy will laugh gladly,
   As he sits on some brave comrade's knee.
But there's one will be true to her duty,
   Who will mourn for the lost and the brave,
As when first in the bloom of her beauty,
   She wept o'er her loved soldier's grave.

LONG LIVE THE GREAT AND FREE.

BY ROBERT M. HART.

(Air:—" Ellen Bane.")

Shrine of devotion!
Far o'er the ocean
Sounds the loud welcome for all to our home;
Millions cross the briny tide,
For those blessings oft denied—
Long live the great and free for ages to come.

CHORUS—Shout for freedom loud and long!
   Let each patriot join the song—
   May Columbia ever boast
   Of *George Washington!*

Fruits, fields and flowers,
Green lawns and bowers,
Yielding their fragrance and bountiful store,
Ever bless this happy land,
Leading on a joyous band—
Long live the great and free to praise and adore.
   CHORUS.—Shout for freedom, &c.

" Faith, love and duty,
Grace and its beauty,"
Be this our motto, and flourish we must!
Freedom then will shine afar
As our nation's chosen star—
Long live the great and free, God is our trust.
   CHORUS.—Shout for freedom, &c.

Wave on in glory—
Bright be thy story,
Flag of Columbia! pure gem of the west
May thy victories ever be:
Peace, good will and harmony—
Long live the great and free, happy and blest.
   CHORUS.—Shout for freedom, &c.

Our *Union* forever!
Naught can dissever:
Bright constellation of unfading ray,
May thy splendor ever beam—
Idol of the patriot's dream—
   CHORUS.—Shout for freedom, &c.

DOWN THE RIVER.

Oh! the river is up, and the channel is deep,
 And the wind blows steady and strong;
Let the splash of your oars the measure keep,
 As we row the old boat along.
Oh! the water is bright, and splashing like gold,
 In the ray of the morning sun,
And old Dinah's away up out of the cold,
 A getting the hoe-cake done.
Oh! the river is up, and the channel is deep,
 And the wind grows steady and strong:
Let the splash of your oars the measure keep,
 As we row the old boat along.

CHORUS.

 Down the river, down the river,
 Down the Ohio;
 Down the river, down the river,
 Down the Ohio.
 Chorus repeated.

Oh! the master is proud of the old broad-horn,
 For it brings him plenty of tin;
Oh! the crew they are darkies, the cargo is corn,
 And the money comes tumbling in.
There is plenty on board for the darkies to eat,
 And there's something to drink and to smoke;
There's the banjo, the bones and the tamborine,
 There's the song and the comical joke.
Oh! the river is up, and the channel is deep,
 And the wind blows steady and strong;
Let the splash of your oars the measure keep,
 As we row the old boat along.

 CHORUS.—Down the river, &c.

OLD FOLKS AT HOME.

Way down on the Swanee ribber,
　Far, far away,
Dere's wha my heart is turning ebber,
　Der's wha de old folks stay.
And up and down the whole creation,
　Sadly I roam;
Still longing for de old plantation,
　And for de old folks at home.

Chorus—All de world am sad and dreary,
　　　　Ebry where I roam;
　　　　Oh! darkies, how my heart grows weary,
　　　　Far from de old folks at home.

All round de little farm I wandered,
　When I was young;
Den many happy days I squandered,
　Many de songs I sung.
When I was playing wid my brudder,
　Happy was I;
Oh! take me to my kind old mudder,
　Dere let me live and die.

Chorus.—All de world am sad and dreary, &c.

One little hut among de bushes,
　One dat I love,
Still sadly to my memory rushes,
　No matter where I rove.
When will I see de bees a humming,
　All round de comb?
When will I hear de banjo tumming,
　Down in my good old home?

Chorus.—All de world am sad and dreary, &c.

THE DRUMMER OF ANTIETAM.

(*Air.—"The Last Rose of Summer."*

The drummer of Antietam,
  Lays, dead and alone,
Upon the cold battle-field,
  Where his blood hath flown;
No friends mourn around him,
  No comrades are near,
To lament his early fate,
  Or o'er him shed a tear.

Now the moon faintly beams,
  On the spot where he lays,
Making his features more ghastly,
  With its misty rays;
While hundreds sleep near him,
  In death's icy chain,
Who've fought their last battle,
  Who'll ne'er wake again.

And thus are the brave,
  Cut off in their bloom,
And manhood's hopes crushed
  In the cold tomb!
But they shall be cherished,
  In the hearts of the free,
As true martyrs of justice,
  And sweet Liberty.

THE BANNER OF THE FREE.

God bless the banner of the free,
   The flag our fathers gave us—
The stars and stripes on land and sea—
   God bless our flag and save us.
For where our country in her might,
   Bears up that flag above us,
We strike for God and for the right,
   Our homes and those that love us.

Chorus—Float forever in the skies,
      Freedom's starry banner!
    Shout, where'er that banner flies,
      Liberty's Hosanna!
    Liberty to all the race,
      Freedom now and ever,
    Here be freedom's dwelling place—
      This her flag for ever!

The names that star the nations on,
   To break the tyrants fetters,
Are written, all its folds upon,
   In never fading letters—
And publish there, in words of light,
   The triumphs of our story.
While beams from all its hues so bright
   The radiance of our glory.
       Chorus.—Float forever, &c.

The pilgrim here, from every clime,
   Beneath that flag rejoices—
And endless years of coming time
   Shall echo to its voices.
Free soil, free men, free faith, free speech,
   O'er all our lands and waters,
The Stars and Stripes shall ever teach
   To all our sons and daughters.

CHORUS.—Float forever, &c.

Then for our flag, Hurrah! Hurrah!
And for the man who bore it,
Till all the foes of light and land,
Are overthrown before it,
And now they're coming up once more,
Though daily growing weaker,
Seeing their leaders toasting now,
The *Union* in full beaker.

CHORUS.—Float forever, &c.

A SOLDIER TO-NIGHT IS OUR GUEST.

Fan, fan the gay hearth, and fling back the barr'd door,
Strew, strew the fresh rushes around on the floor,
And blithe be the welcome in every breast,
For a soldier—a soldier to-night is our guest.

All honor to him, who, when danger afar
Had lighted for ruin his ominous star,
Left pleasures and country, and kindred behind,
And sped to the shock on the wings of the wind.

If you value the blessings that shine at our hearth—
The wife's smiling welcome, the infant's sweet mirth—
While they charm us at eve, let us think upon those
Who have bought with their blood, our domestic repose.

Then share with a soldier your hearth and your home,
And warm be your greeting whene'er he shall come;
Let love light a welcome in every breast,
For a soldier—a soldier to-night is our guest.

THE FLAG OF THE FREE.

Nobly our flag flutters o'er us to-day,
  Emblem of peace, Pledge of Liberty's sway;
Its foes shall tremble and shrink in dismay,
  If e'er insulted it be!
Our Stripes and Stars, loved and honored by all,
  Shall float forever where freedom may call;
It still shall be the Flag of the Free,
  Emblem of sweet Liberty!

CHORUS.

Here we will gather its cause to defend;
  Let Patriots rally and wise counsel lend;
It still shall be the Flag of the Free,
  Emblem of sweet Liberty!

With it in beauty no flag can compare;
  All nations honor our banner so fair.
If to insult it a traitor should dare,
  Crushed to the earth let him be!
Freedom and progress our watchword to-day:
  When duty calls, who dares disobey?
Honor to Thee, Thou Flag of the Free,
  Emblem of sweet Liberty!

CHORUS.—Here we will gather, &c.

MOTHER KISSED ME IN MY DREAM.

A young soldier who was severely wounded at the battle of Antietam, lay at one of the hospitals at Frederick. A surgeon passing by his bed-side, and seeing his boyish face lighted up with a peaceful smile. asked him how he felt. "Oh ! I am happy and contented now," the soldier replied, "last night, mother kissed me in my dream ! "

Lying on my dying bed,
  Through the dark and silent night,
Praying for the coming day,
  Came a vision to my sight;
Near me stood the forms I loved,
  In the sunlight's mellow gleam;
Folding me unto her breast,
  Mother kissed me in my dream;
      Mother, Mother,
      Mother kissed me in my dream!

Comrades, tell her, when you write,
  That I did my duty well;
Say that, when the battle raged,
  Fighting in the van I fell;
Tell her, too, when on my bed,
  Slowly ebbed my being's stream,
How I knew no peace until
  Mother kissed me in my dream.
          Mother, mother, &c.

Once again I long to see
  Home and kindred far away;
But I feel I shall be gone
  Ere there dawns another day!
Hopefully I bide the hour
  When will fade life's feeble beam,
Every pang has left me now,
  Mother kissed me in my dream!
          Mother, mother, &c.

WE'VE DRANK FROM THE SAME CANTEEN.

BY MILES O'RILEY, EDITOR OF "NEW YORK CITIZEN."

There are bonds of all sorts in this world of ours,
Fetters of friendship and ties of flowers,
  And true lovers' knots, I ween.
The boys and girls are bound by a kiss,
But there's never a bond, old friend, like this:
  We have drank from the same canteen.

CHORUS—The same canteen, my soldier friend,
        The same canteen;
      There's never a bond like this:
      We have drank from the same canteen.

It was sometimes water and sometimes milk,
Sometimes applejack, fine as silk;
  But whatever the tipple has been,
We shar'd it together in bane or in bliss,
And I warm to you, friend, when I think of this:
  We have drank from the same canteen.
              CHORUS.—The same canteen, &c.

The rich and the great sit down to dine,
And quaff to each other in sparkling wine,
  From glasses of crystal and green;
But I guess in their golden potations they miss,
The warmth of regard, to be found in this:
  We have drank from the same canteen.
              CHORUS.—The same canteen, &c.

We've shared our blankets and tents together,
And marched and fought, in all kinds of weather,
  And hungry and full we've been;
Had days of battle and days of rest,
But this memory I cling to and love the best:
  We have drank from the same canteen.
              CHORUS.—The same canteen, &c.

For when wounded I lay on the outer slope,
With my blood flowing fast, and but little hope
  On which my faint spirit might lean;
O! then I remember, you crawl'd to my side,
And bleeding so fast, it seemed both must have died,
  We drank from the same canteen.

> CHORUS.—The same canteen, &c.

ELLSWORTH.

Hark to the trumpet' shrill calling,
It pierces the soft summer's air,
Tears from each Zouave is falling,
For the brave, gallant Ellsworth was there.

CHORUS.

Thy bayonets are earthward turning.
And the drum's muffled breath rolls around;
But he hears not the voice of the mourning,
Nor awakes to the bugle's sound.

Ellsworth, why did thy country call thee?
It needed the true and the brave,
Why did this evil befall thee?
Why shrouded thy form for the grave.

> CHORUS.—The bayonets, &c.

Sleep Ellsworth, now a nation mourns thee,
The first to depart to the fray;
Long ere this nation shall forget thee,
Or thy name from the earth pass away.

> CHORUS.—The bayonets, &c.

AND SO WILL THE BOYS IN BLUE.

The bugle call rings loud and clear,
  And loud the rolling drum;
Our comrades haste to seek their posts,
  The time for work has come;
The beacon fires burn bright again,
  They flash on every hill;
From sea to sea the shout goes up,
  We march to victory still!
CHORUS—Hurrah! hurrah! for our noble cause!
    Hurrah for our leaders true!
  We'll stand by the men who stood by the flag,
    And so will the Boys in Blue.
  And so will we all, and so will we all,
    Our pledge we now renew;
  We'll strike once more for the cause we love,
    And so will the Boys in Blue!

Through gloomy years of bloody strife,
  We've battled side by side;
With brave, true hearts and sinewy arms
  We've stemmed each fi'ry tide.
Eternal Justice nerv'd us then,
  And give the conquering will;
With hearts aflame, and God our trust,
  We strike for Justice still.
        CHORUS.—Hurrah, hurrah, &c.
Our motto, equal rights to all;
  The ballot shall be free;
Who stakes his life to save the flag,
  May vote with you and me.
We'll ask him not his birth or kin,
  Or prate about his hue,
But every man unstained with crime,
  May vote with Boys in Blue.
        CHORUS.—Hurrah, hurrah, &c.

THE RETIRED SOLDIER.

The retired soldier, bold and brave,
  Now rests his weary feet,
And in the shelter of the grave,
  ·Has found a safe retreat;
To him the trumpet's piercing breath,
  To arms, they call in vain;
For quartered in the arms of death,
  He'll never, never march again.

CHORUS—March, march again, march, march again,
    March, march again, march, march again,
    For quartered in the arms of death,
    He'll never, never march again.

A day when he left his father's home,
  The charms of war to try,
O'er regions hath he had to roam,
  No friend or mother nigh,
But still he marched contented on,
  Met danger, death and pain,
And now at rest, all danger's o'er,
  He'll never, never march again.

CHORUS.—March, march, &c.

The sweets of spring by beauteous hand,
  Lay scattered on his bier,
Whilst listening round his comrades stand,
  Gave honest Ned a tear,
Whilst lovely Kate, for Ned's delight,
  Chief mourner of the train,
Cried, as she viewed the solemn sight,
  He'll never, never march again.

CHORUS.—March, march, &c.

COLUMBIA'S APPEAL.

(*Air.*—"*Vive La Compagnie.*")

Come all ye true Union men rally again,
    Gather, my boys in blue!
And all the sweet maidens wake up the dear men,
    Gather, my boys in blue!

CHORUS -Gather, gather, gather again!
    Gather, gather, gather again!
    Gather again!   Gather again!
    Gather my boys in blue!

Let none of my enemies call in my name!
    Gather my boys in blue!
Come as when Sumpter guns called you, you came,
    Gather my boys in blue!

            CHORUS.—Gather, &c.

Come, and again win Columbia's thanks,
    Gather, my boys in blue!
Follow Old Glory and fill up the ranks,
    Gather, my boys in blue!

            CHORUS.—Gather, &c.

Sure that you love me, I call upon you,
    Gather my boys in blue!
You who have ever been loyal and true,
    Gather my boys in blue!

            CHORUS.—Gather, &c.

Deep in your hearts your best love is for me,
    Gather my boys in blue!
Shall not your country forever be free?
    Gather my boys in blue!

            CHORUS.—Gather, &c.

They who have sowed should the good harvest reap,
    Gather my boys in blue!
They who have won will the prize safely keep,
    Gather, my boys in blue!

             CHORUS.—Gather, &c.

Truth shall go forward my army to lead,
    Gather, my boys in blue!
Union to help him, and both will succeed,
    Gather, my boys in blue!

             CHORUS.—Gather, &c.

THE FLAG OF OUR UNION.

" A song for our Banner," the watchword recall,
    Which gave the Republic her station,
United we stand, divided we fall!
    It made and preserved us a nation.
The union of lakes, the union of lands,
    The union of states none can sever;
The union of hearts, the union of hands,
    And the Flag of our union forever and ever!
The flag of the Union forever!

What God in His infinite wisdom designed,
    And armed with republican thunder,
Not all the earth's despots and factions combined,
    Have the power to conquer or sunder:
The union of lakes, the union of lands,
    The union of states none can sever:
The union of hearts, the union of hands,
    And the flag of the Union forever and ever;
The flag of the Union for ever!

OUR BOY IS A WARRIOR NOW.

Go brave heart, and say "Good bye."
   Think when the clarion note is heard,
Of our lov'd Washington, and try
   Be brave and prompt, at the battle word.
Your Mother bids you go, dear lov'd one,
   Our holy precepts remember now,
God of Battle will watch o'er thee,
   Go, my boy, be a warrior now.

Chorus—Our hearts are sad, good bye, good bye,
      Think of our country and manly vow;
      God of Battle, will watch o'er thee,
      O'er our boy that's a warrior now.

Our boy when he left us, said:
   A brave soldier, dear mother, I'll be,
Fear not, for one that's above,
   Will watch over our dear country and me.
If in defence of right, I die,
   Lay with me the flag, that now I vow
To hold, while strength in me doth lie,
   For your boy is a warrior now.

               Chorus.—Our hearts, &c.

Will this dread strife never end,
   'Twixt brothers dear and kindred so near?
Will our hearts ne'er cease to ache,
   With cruel doubts and anxious fear.
For brave hearts that have left their homes,
   Who have forsaken the Pen and Plough,
To fight for country and her rights,
   With our boy that's a warrior now.

               Chorus.—Our hearts, &c.

THE SWORD OF BUNKER HILL.

Copied by permission of Russell & Tolman, 291 Washington St.,
Boston, owners of the copyright.

He lay upon his dying bed,
  His eye was growing dim,
When with a feeble voice he call'd,
  His weeping son to him:
"Weep not, my boy," the veteran said,
  " I bow to Heaven's high will,
But quickly from yon antlers bring, } Repeat.
  The sword of Bunker hill."

The sword was brought, the soldier's eye
  Lit with a sudden flame;
And as he grasp'd the ancient blade,
  He murmur'd Warren's name;
Then said, " My boy, I leave you gold,
  But what is richer still,
I leave you, mark me, mark me, now, } Repeat.
  The sword of Bunker hill.

" 'Twas on that dread, immortal day,
  I dared the Briton's band,
A captain raised this blade on me,
  I tore it from his hand;
And while the glorious battle raged,
  It lighten'd freedom's will,
For, boy, the God of Freedom bless'd } Repeat.
  The sword of Bunker hill.

"Oh! keep the sword," his accents broke,
  A smile, and he was dead;
But his wrinkled hand still grasp'd the blade,
  Upon that dying bed.
The son remains, the sword remains,
  Its glory growing still,
And twenty millions bless'd the sire } Repeat.
  And sword of Bunker hill.

7

BRAVE BOYS ARE THEY.

Heavily falls the rain,
 Wild are the breezes to-night;
But 'neath the roof the hours, as they fly,
 Are happy and calm and bright;
Gathering round the fire-side,
 Though it be summer time,
We sit and talk of brot ers abroad,
 Forgetting the midnight chime.

CHORUS—Brave boys are they,
 Gone at their country's call;
 And yet, and yet we cannot forget
 That many brave boys must fall.

Under the homestead roof,
 Nestled so cozy and warm,
While soldiers sleep with little or naught
 To shelter them from the storm,
Resting on grassy couches,
 Pillowed on hillocks damp;
Of martial fare how little we know,
 Till brothers are in the camp!
 CHORUS.—Brave boys are they, &c.

Thinking no less of them,
 Loving our country the more,
We sent them forth to fight for the flag,
 Their fathers before them bore,
Though the great tear-drops started,
 This was our parting trust;
God bless you! boys: we'll welcome you home,
 When rebels are in dust.
 CHORUS.—Brave boys are they, &c.

May the bright wings of love
 Guard them wherever they roam,
The time has come when brothers must fight,
 And sisters must pray at home.
Oh! the dread field of battle—
 Soon to be strewn with graves!
If brothers fall, then bury them where
 Our banner in triumph waves!
 CHORUS.—Brave boys are they, &c.

SLAVERY HAS FALLEN.

Don't you see de black clouds
Rising ober yonder,
Where de massa's ole plantation am;
Neber you he frightened,
Dem is only darkies,
Come to jine and fight for Uncle Sam.

CHORUS—Look out dar now,
We's gwine to shoot,
Look out dar, don't you understand?
Slavery has fallen, slavery has fallen,
An' we's a gwine to occupy de land.

Don't you see de lightning
Flashing in de canebrake,
Like as if we's gwine to hab a storm?
No, you is mistakin,
'Tis de darkies bayonets,
An' de buttons on dar uniforms.

CHORUS.—Look out dar, &c.

Way up in de cornfield,
Where you hear it tunder,
Dat is our ole forty-pounder gun;
When de shells am missen,
Den we lode wid pumpkins,
All de same to make de cowards run.

CHORUS.—Look out dar, &c.

Massa was de Kernel
In de Rebel army,
Eber since he went and run away;
But his lobely darkies,
Da has been a watchen,
And da take him prisoner tudder day.

CHORUS.—Look out dar, &c.

We will be de massa,
He will be de sarvant,
Try him how he like it for a spell;
So we crack de butternuts,
So we take de kernel,
So de cannon carry back de shell.

CHORUS.—Look out dar, &c.

THE DRUMMER BOY OF SHILOH.

On Shiloh's dark and bloody ground,
  The dead and wounded lay;
Among them was a drummer boy,
  Who beat the drum that day.
A wounded soldier held him up,
  His drum was by his side;
He clasped his hands, then raised his eyes,
  And prayed before he died:

Look down upon the battle-field,
  O Thou, our Heavenly friend!
Have mercy on our sinful souls!—
  The soldiers cried, Amen!
For, gathered round a little group,
  Each brave man knelt and cried—
They listened to the drummer boy,
  Who prayed before he died.

O Mother! said the dying boy,
  Look down from Heaven on me;
Receive me to to thy fond embrace—
  Oh! take me home to thee—
I've loved my country as my God;
  To serve them both I've tried—
He smiled, shook hands—death seized the boy,
  Who prayed before he died.

Each soldier wept, then like a child—
  Stout hearts were they, and brave—
The Flag his winding sheet—God's Book,
  The key unto his grave.
They wrote upon a simple board
  These words: this is a guide
To those who mourn the drummer boy,
  Who prayed before he died.

Ye, Angels 'round the throne of grace,
Look down upon the braves,
Who fought and died on Shiloh's plain,
Now slumbering in their graves.
How many homes made desolate!
How many hearts have sighed!
How many like that drummer boy,
Who prayed, before he died!

MASSA'S IN THE COLD GROUND.

Round de meadows am a ringing
The darkies' mournful song,
While the mocking bird is singing,
Happy as the day is long,
Where the ivy is a creeping,
O'er the grassy mound,
There old massa is a sleeping,
Sleeping in the cold, cold ground.

CHORUS—Down in the corn-field,
Hear that mournful sound,
All the darkies are a weeping—
Massa's in the cold, cold ground.

When the autumn leaves were falling,
When the days were cold,
'Twas hard to hear old massa calling,
Cause he was so weak and old.
Now the orange tree is blooming
On the sandy shore,
Now the summer days are coming,
Massa never calls no more.

CHORUS.—Down in the corn-field, &c.

Massa made the darkies love him,
He always was so kind,
Now they sadly weep above him,
Mourning, for he leave them behind.

BENNY HAVENS, OH.

"BENNY HAVENS" was for many years a contraband seller of liquors and viands to the "West Point Cadets," and in course of time, was expelled from the immediate precincts of the military academy. He then opened a regular establishment a mile or two south of West Point, which has been a favorite place of resort for Cadets on a convivial party, "sans permissione." The lamented O'Brien, formerly a sergeant in the army, was commissioned as a lieutenant in the "Eighth Infantry." Before or while about joining his regiment, he stopped at West Point to visit an early friend of his, the late Major RIPLEY A. ARNOLD, then a first-class Cadet, residing at No. 32, "Rue de Cockloft," in the old North Branch. They made frequent excursions to "Benny's." The song was composed by O'BRIEN, ARNOLD, and others of the class, became, as it is now, and ever will be, extremely popular with all graduates who ever learned the way to "Benny Havens" during their academical course at West Point.

A GRADUATE.

Come, tune your voices comrades, and stand up in a row,
For to singing sentimentally, we are about to go.
In the army there's sobriety, promotion very slow,
So we'll sigh our reminiscences of Benny Havens, Oh!

CHORUS—O! Benny Havens, O! O! Benny Havens, O!
　　　　We'll sigh our reminiscences of Benny Havens, O!
　　　　O! Benny Havens, O! O! Benny Havens, O!
　　　　We'll sigh our reminiscences of Benny Havens, O!

Let us toast our foster father (the Republic as you know,)
Who in the paths of science taught us upwards for to go;
And then the maidens of our land, whose cheeks with roses
　　　glow,　　　　　　　　　　　　　　　　　[Havens, O!
Whose smiles and tears were sung 'mid cheers, at Benny
　　　　　　CHORUS.—O! Benny Havens, &c.

To the ladies of the Empire State, whose hearts and al-
　　　bums too,　　　　　　　　　　　　　　　　　[do,
Bear sad examples of the wrongs that stripling soldiers
We bid a sad adieu, our hearts with sorrow overflow, [vens, O!
Our loves and rhymings had their source at Benny Ha-
　　　　　　CHORUS—O! Benny Havens, &c.

Of the smile-wreathed maids with virgin lips, like roses
    dipped in dew,
Who are to be our better halves we'd like to take a view;
But sufficient to the bridal day is the ill of it, you know,
So we'll cheer our hearts with chorusing old Benny Havens O!
               CHORUS.—O! Benny Havens, &c.

To the ladies of the army, our cups shall overflow!
Companions of our exile, and our shield 'gainst every woe!
We throw the gauntlet in their cause, and taunt the soulless
    foe,
Who'd hesitate to drink to them, and Benny Havens O!
               CHORUS.—O! Benny Havens, &c.

May we never lack a smile for friend, or stern heart for a foe,
May all our paths be pleasantness, wherever we may go!
May the muster-roll of after years report us "statu quo,"
And goodly samples of the age, of Benny Havens O!
               CHORUS.—O! Benny Havens, &c.

Oh remember, gallant comrades, as o'er the past we go,
The ties that must be cut in twain, as o'er life's sea we row!
The hearts that throb in unison must moulder down below,
And laughing lips lie mute that wagg'd at Benny Havens O!
               CHORUS.—O! Benny Havens, &c.

'Tis said by commentators, when to other worlds we go,
We follow the same handicraft we did in this below,
If this be true philosophy (the sexton, he says no),
What days of dance and song we'll have at Benny Havens O!
               CHORUS.—O! Benny Havens, &c.

As the ruby-tinted dahlia owes its purest, brightest glow,
To the warmest rays that Sol can pour upon it here below,
So our hearts acquire new joyousness from brilliant eyes
    that throw
The genial rays upon our souls, and Benny Havens O!
               CHORUS—O! Benny Havens, &c.

WRITE A LETTER TO MY MOTHER.

Words by E. BOWERS.   Music by P. B. ISAACS.

An Officer, captured at the battle of Bull Run, relates the following incident. After our capture, I observed a Federal prisoner tenderly cared for by a rebel soldier. I gleaned, from their convers tion, that they were brothers. The brave boy, while battling for the Union, received his death wound from his own brother, at that time a private in the rebel ranks. Never shall I forget the look of utter despair depicted upon that rebel's face ; the dying boy, with a smile of holy re-ignation, clasped his brother's hand, spoke of their father who was then fighting for their dear old flag, of mother, of home, of childhood—then, requesting his brother to *write a letter to mother*, and imploring him never to divulge the secret of his death, the young hero yielded up his life.

Raise me in your arms, my brother,
    Let me see the glorious sun ;
I am weary, faint and dying,
    How is the battle—lost or won ?
I remember you, my brother,
    Sent to me that fatal dart :
Brother fighting against brother,
    'Tis well—'tis well that thus we part.

CHORUS—Write a letter to my mother,
        Send it when her boy is dead ;
    That he perished by his brother,
        Not a word of that be said.

Father is fighting for the Union,
    And you may meet him on the field :
Could you raise your arm to smite him ?
    Oh ! could you bid that father yield !
He who loved us in our childhood,
    Taught the infant prayers we said !
Brother take from me a warning,
    I'll soon be numbered with the dead.

                CHORUS—Write a letter, &c.

Do you ever think of mother,
  In our home within the glen,
Watching, praying for her children?
  Oh! would you see that home again?
Brother, I am surely dying,
  Keep the secret—for 'tis one,
That would kill our angel mother,
  If she but knew what you had done!

        CHORUS.—Write a letter, &c.

"STAND BY THE FLAG."

Words by JNO. N. WILDER, ESQ.   Music by HENRY TUCKER.

Music of this Song published in the Radical Drum-Call.

Stand by the flag, its folds have streamed in glory;
  To foes a fear, to friend a festal robe,
And spread in rhythmic lines and sacred story,
  Of freedom's triumphs over all the globe.
Stand by the flag, on land and ocean billow;
  By it your fathers stood unmoved and true,
Living defended, dying, from their pillow,
  With their last blessings passed it on to you.

Stand by the flag though death-shots round it rattle
  And underneath its waving folds have met,
In all the dread array of sanguine battle,
  The quiv'ring lance and glitt'ring bayonet.
Stand by the flag, all doubt and treason scorning,
  Believe with courage firm, and faith sublime,
That it will float until th' eternal morning
  Pales in its glories all the lights of time.

OUR FIFER-BOY.

(Air.—"James Bird, or, Dying Californian.")

While the battle hot was raging,
  And the shot and shell did fly,
And smoke around our rigging curling,
  Then I heard a piercing cry.

Close beside me lay our fifer;
  From his bosom spouted blood;
There he lay pierced by a bullet;
  Dying in a crimson flood.

Shipmates, said he, tell my father,
  Tell him I died like a man,
Died in battle for my country,
  While blood, around, in torrents ran.

Tell my mother, gently tell her,
  Lest the news should break her heart;
Tell her that her son will meet her,
  Where we never more shall part.

Oh! how sad I am to leave her!
  How she'll mourn about my loss
Her Charlie never more will greet her,
  Never more the ocean cross!   ·

Tell my sister, (Heaven bless her!)
  That her brother is no more,
Hand in hand, no more we'll ramble,
  On Old Hudson's pleasant shore!

Tell my brother, in the army,
  On Potomac's sunny shore,
That our navy is victorious,
  And we'll be so evermore!

Here he paused—and ceased from talking,
  Gently yielded up his breath;
A heavenly smile lit up his features,
  And his eyes were closed in death!

THE FLAG OF FORT SUMTER.

(*Air.*—"*Star Spangled Banner.*")

O say, have you heard how the Flag of our sires
  Was insulted by traitors, in boastful alliance,
When for Union's dear cause, over Sumter's red fires,
  In front of Rebellion it waved its defiance?
      Over Sumter it flew,
      Over patriots true,
And through all that fierce conflict still dearer it grew.
'Twas the flag of Fort Sumter! we saw it still wave
O'er the heads of the free and the hearts of the Brave!

That banner so bright, it was nailed to its mast,
  As a sign that for Freedom there's still no surrender;
And the staff that up-bore it in battle's dread blast,
  Yet remains to be raised by its gallant defender!
      Over Sumter it flew,
      Over Anderson true,
And through all the dark conflict still dearer it grew.
'Twas the Flag of Fort Sumter! O long may it wave
O'er the heads of the Free and the hearts of the Brave!

When in Union's dear name, freedom's cause to sustain,
  Round our Washington's form, half a million assembled,
In the Statue's proud hand, high unrolled once again,
  Rose the Flag that in danger's front never had trembled!
      Streaming heavenward it flew,
      Over patriots true,
And though torn from the conflict, still dearer it grew.
'Twas the Flag of Fort Sumter! we saw it still wave
O'er the heads of the Free and the hearts of the Brave!

There are fields yet to win, there are conflicts to fight,
  Till the foes of our Union are vanquished forever!
But the flag that was nailed over Sumter's red height,
  From the staff that upheld it no traitors can sever;
      It shall fly as it flew,
      Over patriots true,
Whilst our oaths for the Union beneath we renew;
For the Flag of Fort Sumter in glory shall wave
O'er the heads of the Free and the hearts of the Brave!

THE UNION OATH.

BY A. J. H. DUGANNE.

Music of this Song published in the RADICAL DRUM-CALL.

A voice o'er the land goes forth!
'Tis the voice of a nation free!
To the East and the West and the South and the North,
Rolling on like the sounding sea!
'Tis the voice of the Free!
'Tis the shout of the True,
As they swear by the Flag,
Of the Red, White and Blue.

CHORUS—To be true to the *Union* for ever!
Do you hear what it saith,
By the bugle's breath?
To be true to the *Union* forever.

When Royalty vanquished fled,
And the Patriot's power was born,
We surrounded our flag o'er the graves of our dead,
And the first union oath was sworn!
'Twas the oath of the Free—
'Twas the oath of the True—
And they swore by the Flag,
Of the Red, white and Blue.
CHORUS.—To be true to the *Union*, &c.

Rhode Island the clarion blew,
And Connecticut swelled the blast—
Pennsylvania re-echoed to Jersey's hal'oo,
And to Georgia the war-cry past!
'Twas the cry of the Free—
'Twas the shout of the True;
And they swore by the Flag
Of the Red, White and Blue,
CHORUS.—To be true to the *Union*, &c.

Virginia the crown o'ertrod,
Massachusetts the sceptre broke;
From the brave Carolinas the trump went abroad,
And New York with a shout awoke!
'Twas a shout of the Free!
'Twas a word of the True!
And they swore by the Flag
Of the Red, White and Blue.
CHORUS.--To be true to the *Union,* &c.

COLUMBIA RULES THE SEA.

Words by JOSIAH D. CANNING, "Peasant Bard."
Music by HENRY TUCKER.

The pennon flutters in the breeze,
The anchor comes "apeak,"
"Let fall, sheet home," the briny foam,
And ocean's wastes we seek.
The booming gun speaks our adieu,
Fast fades our native shore.
CHORUS—Columbia free, shall rule the sea,
Britannia ruled of yore.

We go the tempest's wrath to dare,
The billows maddened play,
Now climbing high against the sky,
Now rolling low away,
While *Yankee Oak* bears Yankee hearts,
Courageous to the core.
CHORUS.—Columbia free, &c.

We'll bear her flag around the world,
In thunder and in flame,
The sea-girt isles a wreath of smiles,
Shall form around her name,
The winds shall pipe her peans loud,
The billowy chorus roar.
CHORUS.—Columbia free, &c.

THE BOLD VOLUNTEER.

Air:—"The Bold Soldier Boy."

O, there's no use now in sighing,
   Or crying—
   Or shying—
For traitors are defying
The flag we hold so dear!
     And there's not a girl we love, sir,
     Though timid as a dove, sir,
     That will not cast the glove, sir,
When treason walks so near;
    With all her charms,
    She'll rouse to arms;
    With love's alarms—
      She cries
        Arise!
Your country is in danger, my bold Volunteer!

Oh, there's work, boys, to be done,
   None may shun—
   None will run—
There's a battle to be won
For the land we hold so dear!
     And if one there be who'd falter,
     Or shrink from freedom's altar,
     His end may be a halter.
His meed a felon's bier;
    Whilst far away,
    In Freedom's fray,
    We'll win the day,
      And fly
        On high,
The flag that's left in keeping of the Bold Volunteer!

O! we're off to meet the foemen,—
　　Each yeoman　　　　　　 .
　　A Roman;
Away from the pleasant homes and
The scenes we hold so dear;
　　　　But the hearts we leave behind us
　　　　In memory's ties shall bind us,
　　　　Of kindred to remind us,
And friendship's joys sincere;
　　　　In battle's reel,
　　　　'Mid clash of steel,
　　　　And trumpet's peal,
　　　　　We'll hear,
　　　　　　So clear,
The voices that are praying for the Bold Volunteer!

And when to drum and fife,
　　From the strife,
　　Full of life,
Back to sweetheart and to wife
We shall march with songs of cheer,
　　　　Oh! the joys that then will meet us,
　　　　The smiles that then will greet us,
　　　　The lips that will entreat us,
With kisses doubly dear!
　　　　Such royal pay,
　　　　On victory's day,
　　　　Might make us pray
　　　　　For war,
　　　　　　Once more,
To call again to conflict the Bold Volunteer!

I DREAMED MY BOY WAS HOME AGAIN.

Lonely, weary, broken-hearted,
    As I laid me down to sleep,
Thinking of the day we parted,
    When you told me not to weep;
Soon I dreamed that peaceful Angels
    Hovered o'er the battle-plain,
Singing songs of joy and gladness,
    And my boy was home again.

Chorus—How well I know such thoughts of joy,
        Such dreams of bliss are vain!
    My heart is sad my tears will flow,
        Until my boy is home again.

Tears were changed to loud rejoicings,
    Night was turned to endless day,
Loving birds were sweetly singing,
    Flowers blooming in light array;
Old and young seemed light and cheerful,
    Peace seemed everywhere to reign,
My poor heart forgot its sorrow;
    For, my boy was home again!

            Chorus.—How well I know, &c.

But the dream is past: and with it
    All my happiness is gone:
Cheerful thoughts of joy have vanished,
    I must still in sorrow morn;
Soon may peace with all its blessings,
    Our unhappy land reclaim,
Then my tears will cease their flowing,
    And my boy be home again!

            Chorus.—How well I know, &c.

COMRADES, WE COME ONCE MORE.

FOR DECORATION DAY.

Comrades, we come to you once more,
With only an off'ring of flow'rs;
The fondest of mem'ries still are held
Engraved in these hearts of ours.
Brothers, we come with sweetest flow'rs,
Bedewed with the tears of many sad hours;
Fought thou and died thy country to save,
Earth has no pow'r beyond the grave.

REFRAIN.

Comrades we come to you once more,
With only an off'ring of flow'rs;
The fondest of mem'ries still are held
Engraved in these hearts of ours.

Now as we stand beside your graves,
Our tho'ts turn to days that are past;
So noble and brave you did defend
Our dear country to the last.
Out from your homes, the nations pride;
You fought for the right, you bled and died;
The nation now mourns its soldiers brave,
With flowers we now bedeck your grave.

REFRAIN.—Comrades we come, &c.

8

"THE BRAVE, NOBLE AND TRUE."

DECORATION HYMN.

There's a vacant niche in the heart,
In some shady nook a grave,
A marble to point out the spot,
And tell what that sad heart gave
When our country called for her sons,
The brave, the noble and true,
To defend with their valiant arms,
The precious Red, White and Blue.

REFRAIN.

Brave young heroes now sleeping,
Our hearts are filled with grief, filled with grief;
As these graves this day we're strewing,
With sweet bud, flow'r and leaf.

This morn in sweet, balmy May,
With fragrance of flow'rs so fair,
We greet as the dear, sacred day,
When we to these graves repair;
Where many hearts beat as one,
In sorrow, heart felt and true,
For the brave young heroes now mourn,
Who died for the Red, White and Blue.

REFRAIN.—Brave young heroes, &c.

There's an empty chair in each home,
Folded garments are now laid by,
And a voice tho' now hush'd in the tomb,
Still echoes to us back our sigh;
There's a hope we've laid up in heav'n
For him long passed from our view,
Whose life so freely was giv'n,
To save the Red, White and Blue.

REFRAIN.—Brave young heroes, &c.

God raiseth the lovely flow'rs,
'Tis thus smileth He from above;
And lightens this pathway of ours,
With those sweet tokens of love.
And with loving hands did we weave
These garlands of rainbow hue,
And on the brave hero's grave leave,
The fragrant Red, White and Blue.

   REFRAIN.—Brave young heroes, &c.

HUSHED O'ER THIS SACRED FIELD OF MOUNDS.

MEMORIAL HYMN.

Hushed o'er this sacred field of mounds;
And all the conflict's distant sounds,
Nor roll of drums, nor cannon's roar,
Alarm our silent comrades more!
From darkened homes in sadness borne;
From southern plains all battle torn;
From mountain march, and midnight tramp,
They reached at last this peaceful camp.

By this pure lake, where bud and leaf
Surround the symbols of our grief,
Their graves we strew with May's fair flow'rs,
Whose lives went out to sweeten ours.
So as the spring-times come and end,
And early blossoms blush and bend,
Shall loving footsteps, year by year,
With fresh memorials linger here.

Oh, may some happy spring-time bring
Heaven's blessed calm upon its wing,
When peace shall reign from shore to shore,
And war's red ensign float no more.

BRING MY BROTHER BACK TO ME.

Bring my brother back to me,
When this war is done;
Give us all the joys we shared,
Ere it had begun;
Oh! bring my brother back to me,
Never more to stray!
This is all my earnest prayer,
Through the weary day.

CHORUS—Bring him back, bring him back,
With his smiling, healthful glee;
Bring him back, bring him back,
Bring my brother back to me!

All the house is lonely now,
And my voice no more,
In the pleasant summer eves,
Greets him at the door.
Nevermore I hear his step
By the garden gate,
While I sit in anxious tears,
Knowing not his fate.

CHORUS.—Bring him back, &c.

Bring my brother back to me,
From the battle strife;
Thou who watchest o'er the good,
Shield his precious life!
When this war has passed away,
Safe from all alarms;
Bring my brother home again,
To my longing arms!

CHORUS.—Bring him back, &c.

GOD IS WITH THE RIGHT.

Words by MAURICE BINGHAM.   Music by EMIL STADLER.
The music of this song is published by E. H. Harding, 288 Bowery,
Price 10 cents.

Columbia, land of freedom's birth,
  On many a battle plain,
Thy sons have crush'd the foe to earth,
  It shall be so again.
For when foul Treason rears its head
  And dares assert its right,
Its cohorts yet shall learn to dread,
  The Northmen in their might.

CHORUS.

To arms we fly, and this the cry to nerve us in the fight:
Our cause is just, succeed we must,
  God is with the right.

Though rebel hosts have dared to crave
  Dominion o'er our seas,
Our star speck'd flag alone shall wave
  Triumphant in the breeze.
A million Patriot swords are drawn,
  And scabbards cast aside,
To battle for the Union sworn,
  For which our fathers died.
          CHORUS.—To arms we fly, &c.

A stalwart band of freemen bold
  Arouse at duty's call,
Our Constitution to uphold
  And by it stand or fall;
Ere long again o'er land and main,
  Our glorious flag unfurl'd,
Columbia free once more shall be,
  A beacon to the world,
          CHORUS.—To arms we fly, &c.

HURRAH FOR THE WHITE, RED AND BLUE.

Hush'd is the clamorous trumpet of war,
Hush'd hush'd is the trumpet of war;
The soldier's retired from the clangor of arms,
The drum rolls a peaceful hurrah.
'Tis cheering to think on the past,
'Tis cheering to think we've been true,
'Tis cheering to look on our stars and our stripes,
And gaze on our white, red and blue.
Hurrah for the white, red and blue,
Hurrah for the white, red and blue,
'Tis cheering to look on our stars and our stripes,
And gaze on our white, red and blue.

Here's a sigh for the brave that are dead,
Here's a sigh for the brave that are dead,
And who would not sigh for the glorious brave,
That rest on a patriot bed?
'Tis glory for country to die,
'Tis glory that's solid and true;
'Tis glory to sleep 'neath our stars and our stripes,
And die for our white, red and blue,
Hurrah for the white red and blue,
Hurrah for the white, red and blue,
'Tis glory to sleep 'neath our stars and our stripes,
And die for the white, red and blue.

Here's freedom of thought and of deed,
Here's freedom in valley and plain,
The first song of freedom that rose on our hills,
Our sea-shore re-echoed again.
'Tis good to love country and friends,
'Tis good to be honest and true:
'Tis good to die shouting, on sea or on shore,
"Hurrah for the white, red and blue,"
Hurrah for the white, red and blue,
Hurrah for the white, red and blue,
'Tis good to die shouting, at sea or on shore,
"Hurrah for the white, red and blue!"

SLEEPING FOR THE FLAG.

When our boys come home in triumph, brother,
  With the laurels they shall gain,
When we go to give them welcome, brother,
  We shall look for you in vain.
We shall wait for your returning, brother,
  Though we know it cannot be,
For your comrades left you sleeping, brother,
  Sleeping 'neath that Southern tree.

CHORUS—Sleeping to awaken
        In this weary world no more,
        Sleeping for your true loved country, brother,
        Sleeping for the flag you bore.

You who were the first on duty, brother,
  When, to arms! your leader cried,
You have left the ranks forever, brother,
  You have laid your arms aside.
From the awful scenes of battle, brother,
  You were set forever free,
When your comrades left you sleeping, brother,
  Underneath that Southern tree.

                    CHORUS.—Sleeping to awaken, &c.

You have crossed the clouded river, brother,
  To the mansions of the blest,
Where the wicked cease from troubling, brother,
  And the weary are at rest.
Surely we would not recall you, brother,
  Though we know it cannot be,
When we think of you as sleeping, brother,
  Underneath that Southern tree.

                    CHORUS.—Sleeping to awaken, &c.

TREAD LIGHTLY O'ER THEIR GRAVES.

HYMN FOR DECORATION DAY.

O comrades, bring the choicest flowers
  Of incense breathing May;
With fragrant buds and laurel wreaths,
  We'll deck their graves to-day.
The starry flag o'er many mounds
  Above the low grass waves,
There lightly step 'tis hallowed ground,
  Tread lightly o'er their graves.

REFRAIN.—Step lightly where the starry flag
      Above the low grass waves,
      For there our gallant comrades sleep,
      Tread lightly oe'r their graves,

How well they loved the starry flag,
  Their gallant deeds attest;
They saved their country from her foes,
  And won their honored rest.
Then deck the turf where e'er the flag
  Above the green mound waves,
For there our country's heroes sleep,
  Tread lightly o'er their graves.

REFRAIN.—Step lightly where the starry flag, &c.

While we let fall the tear to-day
  That tells our country's loss,
Far in the East in strife are met
  The Crescent and the Cross.
But peace o'er fair Columbia
  Her olive garland waves,
They bought that peace whose mounds we deck,
  Tread lightly o'er their graves.

REFRAIN.—Step lightly where the starry flag, &c.

UNCLE SAM.

(Air.—Yankee Doodle.)

There is an independent chap that lives this side the water,
To serve or beat a foe, he is a regular snorter;
He keeps an open house to all, to all gives invitation,
To enter in and taste the sweets of freedom wid de nation

In the year of '76, his daddy made him mad, sir,
By trying to impose on him, so he licked his dad, sir;
His daddy's name was Johnny Bull, who at him kept on
      pickin',
Until the year 1812, when he got another lickin',

The Southerners they did secede, so into them he pitches,
And Grant and Sherman down he sends, who licks 'em out
      der britches;
If any other nation tries, while thinking him a noodle,
To tread upon his corns, he'll give him Yankee Doodle.

Although he's young, he's mighty big and daily growing
      bigger,
And if any of you have seen this chap, you can't mistake
      his figure,
His dress is made of stars and stripes, about him there's no
      sham, sir.
For what he says he's bound to do, and that is Uncle Sam,
      sir.

INDEX.

UNION PACIFIC RAILWAY
═══AND CONNECTIONS═══

The Only Lines Across the Plains and Rocky Mountains,

Through the Great Mineral, Pastoral and Agricultural Belts to the
finest Health and Pleasure, Hunting and Fishing
Resorts on the Globe.

COLORADO CITIES AND RESORTS are best reached via the Union Pacific Railway, Colorado Division. Largest cities, richest mines, best hunting, fishing and pleasure resorts are along or in sight of the Colorado Division, and the tourist passing closely along the base of the Rocky Mountains for over 100 miles, is thus afforded a constant and perfect view of the **Grandest Mountain Panorama in the World!** From May to October excursion tickets are sold at very low rates, enabling the tourist to go west by the Union Division and return by the Kansas Division Union Pacific Railway, or vice versa.

BLACK HILLS AND BIG HORN.—The Sidney Stage Line, in connection with the Union Pacific Railway, affords the shortest, quickest, and the only safe and pleasant stage journey to all prominent points in the Black Hills, being the only route open the whole year. By this route, passengers avoid the 200-mile stretch of uninhabitable and almost impassable bad lands, north and east of the Hills, and the depredating bands of savages which regularly infest them.

The Rock Creek and Big Horn Daily Stage Line, connecting with Union Pacific trains at Rock Creek, Wyoming, affords the only means of access to Forts Fetterman, McKinney, Custer, Big Horn City, and all points in the BIG HORN REGION and Southeastern Montana.

MONTANA, UTAH AND IDAHO.—The Union Pacific connects with the Utah & Northern Railway for the Snake and Salmon River Mines, Idaho, as well as Helena, Deer Lodge, Virginia, Butte, Glendale, Bozeman, and all the best Mining and Agricultural Regions in Montana, and with the Utah Central at Ogden for Salt Lake City, Frisco, Leeds, and all points in Utah. There is no other route to the great Salmon River Region, and no other route during fall, winter, or spring, to Montana.

CALIFORNIA, ARIZONA, OREGON AND WASHINGTON.—The Union and Central Pacific Railroads form the only line across the continent, to all points in Nevada, California, Oregon and Washington ; and in connection with the Southern Pacific affording the only rail route to the heart of Arizona ; or in connection with the finest steamship lines, to China, Japan and India.

For information concerning the resources, climate and other attractions of any of the above regions, address,

THOS. L. KIMBALL,
Gen. Pass. and Ticket Agent, OMAHA, NEB.

S. H. H. CLARK, General Manager.

PRESCRIPTION DRUGGISTS,

Fifteenth and Douglas Streets, OMAHA, NEB.

KEEP THE FINEST LINE OF

FANCY GOODS!

The Largest Assortment of Perfumery,

WARRANTED TOOTH BRUSHES.

BOTTLED MINERAL WATER.

McDonald & Harrison

IMPORTERS AND MANUFACTURERS

–OF–

Ladies' Cloaks, Suits and Mantles

At New York prices. A full assortment of

UNDERWEAR AND HOSIERY

Always on hand.

WEDDING OUTFITS A SPECIALTY.

We guarantee a perfect fit in every instance.

Agency for Mme. Demorest's Reliable Patterns.

FURNITURE.

The Oldest and Largest

FURNITURE ESTABLISHMENT IN THE STATE.

OMAHA, NEB.

D. A. PIERCY,

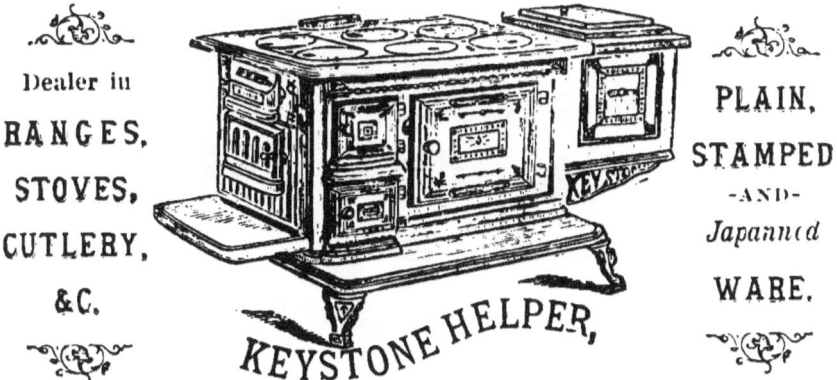

KEYSTONE HELPER,

Dealer in
RANGES,
STOVES,
CUTLERY,
&C.

PLAIN,
STAMPED
-AND-
Japanned
WARE.

HOUSE FURNISHING GOODS & GRANITE IRON WARE

1211 Farnam Street, OMAHA, NEB.

Job Work a Specialty.